THE AIRE OF BROOME PARK

PATRICK KINSMAN

LifeRich Publishing is a registered trademark of
The Reader's Digest Association, Inc.

LifeRich Publishing books may be ordered
through booksellers or by contacting:

LifeRich Publishing
1663 Liberty Drive
Bloomington, IN 47403
www.liferichpublishing.com
844-686-9607

ISBN: 978-1-4897-4112-7 (sc)
ISBN: 978-1-4897-4116-5 (e)

Library of Congress Control Number: 2022906314

Print information available on the last page.

LifeRich Publishing rev. date: 04/01/2022

CONTENTS

DEDICATIONS

I must first thank my Mother, who, like all Mothers, saved early fine art items, created by their children, to give to them in later life. After I had my own children, she gave me assorted items, one of which, was my first written piece of work, a musical play named *Broadway Here We Come*, which I wrote around age 12. I think I composed it after seeing a Mickey Rooney – Judy Garland movie about Kids making a Broadway Play, so I'm guessing it is fraught with plagiarism. For whatever reason, that first piece launched a recurring streak of creativity in me. Over the years I wrote short stories, poems, songs and even another musical. All of these creations accomplished nothing more than giving me something to do, when I had time on my hands.

This book is my first attempt at writing a novel, and in fact, it is an Historical Novel, in which I intertwine my "Father's Side" of my family lineage. Other than the challenge of actually writing and finishing a book, it is dedicated to our five children and their children, and it is meant for them to better understand that lineage. It is also meant to encourage them to find within themselves, "their own fine art talents", as when they were young, all our children had their own streaks of creativity, which led to a Beauty and the Beast production being held live in our living room, as well as other shows, paintings, music and stories being developed by them.

One of the best benefits of developing fine arts, is allowing the brain to "feel free" to create. It becomes exhilarating to the mind when the process of creativity takes place and it is my hope that our Grandchildren can experience true creativity in their lives. Caroline and Ryan, the two oldest, are already developing these talents. I pray the others do it as well, even if it is only for their parents to save their childhood work for them to review after they have grown.

I also want thank my wife, who over the years, has been patient and encouraging with me, as this "creative arm" of my life, took on its' own form.

Lastly, thanks to my dear friend, Jeff Miller,

who was not only one of the first people to read my original draft, he also "completed edited" this work for me. He caught most of my grammatical mistakes and he corrected several of my historical references. All it cost me was to replace his pad of "post it" notes, which covered my manuscript. Thanks again Jeff!

PROLOGUE

Historical Novels have been popular since paper was developed. Stories of the past are interesting to most people, especially if they deal with romantic periods of time in history. Weaving history into a fictional story can be fun for both writer and reader as "anything" becomes possible with the pen.

In the late 1990's, our English relatives sent us copies of old family letters circulated to other relatives in the UK. These letters explained that the eldest daughter of my five-time Great Grandfather, James Kinsman, married into an Aristocratic Family in County Kent England. Through further investigation, my eldest sister, Ruth, and I, traced that family's heritage back to the mid 1300's, to the time of King Edward III of England.

I must admit that this all happened, during the

first year of the popularity of the British Television Drama, Downton Abbey, which became the inspiration for me, to create this story. It is only natural that, just like our English relatives wanted us to know about the history of one of their own, I hope one of the benefits of writing this book, is that my children and grandchildren, and those yet to be born, will have the fun of learning about distant relatives from another time in history, if only to know about what life may have been like for those people, during that time in England.

CHAPTER 1

OUR LAST TWO DAYS IN ENGLAND

The events of this past summer only added to my uncertainty, which existed from the day I first stepped on the grounds of Broome Park. My Uncle Patrick had first told me of this place and insisted I place it on my "bucket list" of places to visit. I thought this rather strange, because he admitted that indeed, he had never been there himself. Still, knowing I was traveling with Lisa for 40 days to see as much of England and Scotland as we could stand, we left the last 2 days of our journey to take in as much of County Kent as time would allow.

We began Friday morning, awakened by the sound of waves coming ashore under the Cliffs of

Dover. Our quaint Bed & Breakfast overlooked the English Channel and with windows open because the previous night had been warm and humid, we had fallen asleep to a quiet stillness, only to be disturbed about 5:00am by the furious curtains, knocking against our night-stand lampshade forcing me to rise to an angry Channel with waves hitting the beach, as though they'd been thrown all the way from France.

I sat by the window, on the small Queen Anne chair, for a few minutes before lowering the sash, taking in the wondrous beauty of nature. The contrast of whites and grays was remarkable. The pure whiteness of the fabled Cliffs, was definitely the focal point of this visual painting, which was balanced by the light gray waters and the dark gray sky, with even darker clouds catching the eye and serving as a stark reminder of how English weather can change so quickly. As I completely closed the window, Lisa sat up in bed and the light coming into our room from outside engulfed her lovely face as though it was a soft white spotlight shining on a stage with only her to receive it. I was indeed a lucky man. Uncle Pat had said it many times, that Lisa had an amazing resemblance to Grace Kelly during her Hollywood Years and after as Princess of Monaco. Having turned 45 in May, she still could pass for 25 and I have always had to admit, that wherever I was with her, she turned heads and gave me the feeling that no one would have noticed me by her side. Still her love for me now, 24 years later, was even stronger than our days at North Park in Chicago.

"Evan? Evan!! Evan?" Her voice disturbed my love fixation and brought me back to the present. "Honey, what are you doing up so early?" "Just shutting the window, dear. It's really windy outside this morning." "Oh, I hope this doesn't affect your golf today. Uncle Pat said you would love the Broome Park Course." "We'll see", I responded, as I climbed back into bed to make love to my beautiful wife before we started the days' activities. Actually, we had been so busy for the past few days, our exhaustion and the oppressive heat and humidity caused us just to collapse every evening, grateful we had made it through our overbooked schedule. While our London and Edinburgh accommodations both had air conditioning, the smaller hotels and B&B's throughout this island somehow wanted their tenants to experience the Britain of old, with sparse lodging, toilet and comforts of home, over which, we Americans have become so spoiled.

This morning and this bedroom would be different. The cool breeze that awoke us was just the ticket to make Lisa snuggle up to me, under the covers. Still, a quarter of a century later, each time with her, was like our Honeymoon; fresh, exciting and filled with so much love, I could barely comprehend how lucky I was to have her in my life. Our three wonderful children were almost 20, 18 and 16, and they were safe, back home in Michigan, and this was the perfect time for them to be with Grandma & Grandpa, while we spent our August in the UK.

Having sold my Seat on the Board of Trade 10 years ago, this allowed me to pursue other business interests, but also gave us the opportunity to enjoy the wonderful blessings, on which God had bestowed upon us. For the past several summers, our vineyard on the West side of Michigan, was our heaven on earth. It was comforting to know that even now, in their late teens, the kids loved living there, apparently even when we were away. Our call to them yesterday was short and sweet, as the weather there was also unbearably hot, which for Michigan, in the late summer, was also unusual. But, knowing the kids could enjoy themselves with lots to do on the farm, was good for them. They would find a way to keep themselves cool. For us, it was not that easy, here on the Dover coast as the Channel lay hundreds of steps below us, and I somehow couldn't imagine this portion of the Atlantic Ocean being as refreshing as a Michigan lake or stream. Still, having Lisa lovingly hover over me for these last few moments of our rising, automatically gave me plenty of memories to add to this wonderful trip.

Gleneagles, the site of the 2014 Ryder Cup, and the Old Course at St. Andrews were the only two golfing stops, during our first 28 days of travel. Just as Uncle Pat had done in 2001, when he and Aunt Katherine had their tour of the British Isles, he said, "You don't need to bring your own golf clubs, but just your shoes, as both great venues for golf, would have great clubs to rent", for me to at least add to my golfing bucket list. He was correct. Though I didn't play very well, it didn't matter, as the enjoyment of playing in Scotland, and especially at St. Andrews, is just experiencing a walk through history. The Town of St. Andrews was one of Lisa's favorite spots to see thus far, as meandering through this ancient village was precisely the kind of experience she wanted to encounter.

Reflecting on that, I could not imagine what I was to encounter, hours from now, as what lay ahead at Broome Park still remains a mystery.

After breakfast, we headed North on the M-8 in our Ryan Air Rental Car. The flatness of the countryside from Dover to Canterbury, would be disturbed every so often with some gentle rolling hills, but for the most part, Southeastern England, was much like Southeastern Michigan. Once outside the cities, it was green, flat, with enough vegetation to make the drive not so boring. Lisa was looking forward to her day in Canterbury. She loved history and her anticipation of this magnificent part of English lore was just what was needed to entertain her for the 6 hours or so that would require me to go and play Broome Park Golf Course and get back North to County Kent's most famous city. Why Uncle Patrick wanted me to play this course in particular, I did not fully understand, other than the fact, that some of our distant relatives were related to the Oxenden Family, which inhabited the Estate at

Broome Park, since it was built in the mid sixteen hundreds.

Canterbury was less than 25 kilometers North of Broome Park, so when I dropped off Lisa at 9:30am, she said, "Don't hurry Evan. Have fun. I will meet you right here at 5:00pm or so. Enjoy playing, even if it is just for the memory of Uncle Pat." Why she said that I have no idea, but as I went back South on the M8, all I could think of was Uncle Pat. My mother's only brother was like another Father/Brother to me. Only 19 years my senior, during our formative years, he would play every imaginable game with my Brother, Ethan, 3 years my Junior, and my Cousin Thomas, one year younger than me, with whom I played, vacationed and was as close to, as I was to Ethan. Uncle Pat was a fabulous athlete who loved playing basketball against us all, even during our High School days, when Thomas and I were high school teammates. Actually, a few times I would get frustrated playing against him, as his defense was so intense, once, out of frustration that I couldn't drive past him or score against him, I said, "Uncle Pat, nobody plays defense as hard as you do." His response was, "Great then, because if you can get by me, you can get by anyone and score at will against any opponent." Still, for an adult to make it so tough for a 15-year old to have some fun at driveway basketball, indicated how intently he played all sports. He approached virtually any past time with the same intensity, whether sports, music, vacationing or just going to the movies, everything with Uncle Patrick, was an adventure to be conquered.

When he first shared with me, the historical details of Broome Park, I was amazed that he had uncovered so much information that certainly wasn't easily available, even on the internet. Although there is a real family connection to this old English Estate, our collective family couldn't lay much claim to the legacy and heritage of the Oxenden lineage, except for the eldest daughter of my Mother's/Uncle's Great Great Great Great Grandfather, James Tanner, who was raised as a "Gentleman", meaning he didn't need to work for a living, in Southern England, close to the South Coast beach town of Brighton. When and where Elizabeth Phoebe Tanner first met, Sir Henry Chudleigh Oxenden, the 8th Baronet in the Baronetcy of the Oxenden Family, which dates back to the mid 1300's, is anyone's guess. Uncle Pat, through family letters dating back to the late 1800's, was able to confirm that Sir Henry, who after his first wife Charlotte had died, leaving Sir Henry with 4 young children to raise on his own, must have come across the young maiden, Elizabeth, and began a romance that resulted in an 1848 wedding, near London, at the historic St. George's Church, in Hanover Square, Westminster, Middlesex, England. While it wasn't a Royal Wedding, it at least must have had some sense of a High Society occasion, to have taken place 75 miles from Broome Park.

Whom ever attended the wedding and wherever they spent their honeymoon is anyone's guess, but eventually they ended up in the center of Kent County, 8 miles North of Dover, which was coming closer with each passing minute on the M8. I couldn't help but wonder how Sir Henry and Elizabeth got to Broome Park from London in the mid-19th Century. What route did they take? Were the roads of 1848 routed the same as today's concrete thoroughfares? Or, were there more direct routes, which would cut the time it took to go from London to Canterbury to Broome Park, with paths winding through the dozens of small hamlets that must have dotted the Southeastern English countryside during the reign of Queen Victoria.

What a sight it must have been for the peasants of each village as the Oxenden carriage come through the center of town. Did they bow or curtsy? Were they even allowed to look directly at the Upper Class back then? What did they do for a living? Probably they were farmers. What else could they have done? This was England just before the dawn of the Industrial Revolution. Unless you were in service to an upper class family, or employed at the workhouses around London, or a fisherman on the coast, farming pretty much was your only choice. I guess.

Anyways, as the sign to Broome Park Golf Course steered me West off the highway, my excitement about seeing this semi-legendary Estate began to rise. What was it that Uncle Patrick wanted me to experience here? He stated that the golf course wasn't going to rank with St. Andrews or Pebble Beach, but still probably fun to play with most holes having a different view of the 4-story high, 45 room, Broome Park edifice, whose entrance was now in front of me. Turning into the brick protected, prior private road, which now served as the publics' access to this former Estate, turned 5 Star Hotel/Condominum complex, with surrounding 18-hole golf layout, was now within in eyesight.

Wow! Great Aunt Elizabeth Phoebe really hit the jackpot when she married good old Sir Henry Chudleigh Oxenden. The virtually square shaped edifice was indeed 4 stories high, but it looked like only storage was beyond the 3rd floor, rather than additional rooms. The symmetry of the building was also very striking, with multiple chimneys protruding from various points on the roof. I'm not sure what kind of architecture was in vogue in 1643, but "lavish simplicity" is what I would call Broome Park. The main entrance could be driven up to on white crushed gravel, as opposed to a concrete or blacktop driveway. I'm guessing the gravel driveway was still the way it was when Aunt Elizabeth lived here.

Except for the golf carts and trolleys that were gathered around one corner of the building, near the Pro Shop portion of the complex, you couldn't tell this was anything but an old Manor Home, rather than a building with Condominiums, Hotel Rooms, an indoor Pool, a restaurant, exercise room, the Golf Pro Shop, and assorted Ballrooms, now used for Locals seeking a nice venue for Wedding Receptions. It still looked every bit like a home for extreme English Upper Class.

Well, now it was time for the American to find out what lay in store, inside of Broome Park, as well as the Golfing grounds that surrounded the property's focal point. Uncle Pat was right when he said the golf course wasn't anything special, at least at first glance it wasn't. With a pretty flat terrain, dotted with some minor forests, and a couple of strategically placed ponds to catch errant or not well enough hit golf shots, the course seemed to be just an additional attraction to the Resort Guests, who now like me, were more intrigued with what lay inside these light reddish brown bricks and cultured windows, that adorned the building.

Driving up to the un-bordered, smallish parking lot, also made of gravel, I then noticed the small Golf Shop sign on the East Wall. The proprietors were doing all they could to ensure Broome Park's charm was not too disturbed when they transitioned the Estate from a Residence to a Public House, complete with the many amenities that both English and European Travelers would want in a Holiday spot. I don't think they even considered what American Travelers would want in our Vacation Retreats, as this quality a building in the USA would have a "entrance area", lavishly bestowed with richly looking statues, fountains, red carpets and bell captains, all waiting to serve any visitor with a "Welcome to our Humble Abode", at only $495 per night; golf extra. Broome Park did have the same financial expectations as any J.W. Marriott might have, with 390 lbs. Sterling being the daily rate, with golf at a modest 125 lbs. per round; caddies and/ or cart extra.

After parking my pitiful rental car in between an Astin Martin and a new Jaguar on one side, and a Bentley and C Class Mercedes on the other side, it started to dawn on me, how successful were the Broome Park owners in attracting a clientele that didn't really care what the night or weeks lodging, food and entertainment were going to cost them. For them, Broome Park was an escape from their boring lives in East Piccadilly, Hyde Park or the Regents' Park sections of greater London where they were bringing their wives or mistresses.

As I walked by the golfers readying themselves for the first hole, polite British smiles greeted me as I walked past them into the building. While the inside was definitely a Golf Shop, it was the first I had seen with 16 foot high ceilings, with huge crown moldings around the top, and wainscoted walls showing wherever not blocked by glass display cases filled with, for sale golf clothing, golf balls and gloves and assorted other niceties all earmarked for buyers with lots of disposable income.

It's not like I'm a pauper, having basically been retired since my early forties, but I can't imagine paying 200 lbs. for a Pringle Argyle sweater, not even in Scotland. As the desk was busy with would be golfers, and the fact that I had arrived much earlier than my 11:00 tee time, I wandered through the Pro Shop and found myself in the what looked to be a continuation of the Pro Shop rooms, with the same 16 foot ceilings. As they converted this small castle into its' Resort of today, I could see walls had been created to separate some of the rooms from one another. Perhaps 380 years ago, this rooms' original purpose was as a Ballroom, complete with Glass Chandeliers, huge wall mirrors and wooded floors used to waltz guests around during formal parties.

Walking further towards the front and center of Broome Park, I encountered multiple small rooms, now turned into private dining areas or meeting rooms. What they were when first built, I can only guess. I'm sure the Servants' Quarters were in the basement, or around the back of the house. House, I laughed as I thought of this as a house where one family would live. Lisa and I had been through Windsor and Edinburgh's Castles this month, and certainly they were even more spectacular than Broome Park, but they had been built to house Royalty. This was just a home for some wealthy, well connected English Family. It looked similar, but not quite as large as the Highclere Castle home, which was used in the British Television Series, Downton Abbey, during the years from 2010 – 2015. However, the original proprietors of Broome Park, I would find out later, actually knew the family from Highclere.

Uncle Pat had given me the detail of the lineage of the Oxenden Baronetcy, which began with the 1st Baronet, who attained Knighthood in the 1500s, but the Oxenden family name goes back to England during the reign of Edward III. Why the original Solomon Oxendin, spelled his name differently in 1240, as compared to the last 8 of 10 generations we could not discover. As I walked through what was now the Lobby of Broome Park,

I recognized the fireplace and walls from a picture of the estate which Uncle Pat had shown me years ago. I could see the paneled places on either side of the tall fireplace, where pictures of Sir Henry and his relations, down through the years, had been sort of enshrined for future generations, as was the case in any castle throughout Europe, and particularly, here in England. I imagined Aunt Elizabeth first walking into her new home and what she must have thought to have then been a part of its' lineage.

The craftsmanship of the original décor was still very much in tact as everywhere had been preserved as much of the Oxenden home as was possible. Richly carved doorways still welcomed occupants who walked from room to room. I was now standing, in what appeared to be the family dining room; rectangular in shape with again the high ceilings and much adorned walls and floors. I guessed that as many as 40 to 50 could have easily been hosted for a meal, with still plenty of room for the servers to walk around the lengthy table that might have been placed at the rooms' center. Now in the 21st Century, the room was filled with tables for four with chairs, linens and dinner ware neatly ready for any guest and any meal.

Looking out the windows of that room, I engaged the view that the Oxenden's must have enjoyed every day, looking South towards Dover, with Gardens to the left and rows of trees lining the road up which, I had just driven. To the right I could see some gentle rolling hills and noticed some of the green fairways, with assorted golfers already enjoying their round. As I made my way to the center front of the building, I reached the Foyer, with even higher ceilings over the not so massive, heavy wooden, front door, which was flanked by two narrow but tall glass panes, measuring, I say, about 15 feet in height. Turning inward towards the staircase, it wasn't quite as wide as Rhett and Scarlett Butler's Atlanta home red carpeted stairs, but none the less, it gave a grand presence to the Foyer, as I imagined how Sir Henry and Aunt Elizabeth must have greeted their numerous guests over the years.

Looking at my watch, I realized I would have to take in the rest of the House after my round, as I made my way back to the Pro Shop to purchase my green fee and rent my clubs and trolley. I didn't want a cart, as I wanted to take in as much of the terrain on foot as possible, if only to get a feel for what a walk around the estate must have felt like 165 years ago.

Walking through the Pro Shop portal, I made eye contact with the pretty clerk, standing behind the counter, who smiled back at me, as I said, "Christian, the 11:00am Tee Time?" "Of course, Mr. Christian, welcome to Broome Park," was her courteous reply. Taking my credit card she mentioned, "Your reservation says, rental clubs included, I do hope a set of Callaway's will meet with your approval." "Yes, that's fine. Thank you." I commented back. Handing me back my credit card and receipt, she explained, "We have you paired with Mr. and Mrs. Witherington, who have already played once this weekend. You will enjoy them immensely and they have been here many times before, so they will be able to share with you our course layout. They too, are walkers, pulling their bag trolleys." Noticing her name tag, I said, "Thank you Olivia." And then I walked out the door, to my car, where I changed my shoes and proceeded to the starters' booth, and handed over my ticket to the quite tall, Mr. Abernathy. "Good morning sir. Yes, Mr. Christian, sir." He replied, in a British Military manner. He continued, "We have you playing with Mr. & Mrs. Witherington, sir."

"None of that stuffy stuff Mr. Abernathy, it is just plain Charles and Penelope, Mr. Christian," were the words I heard to my left from the obvious Mr. Witherington. Hand outstretched, he continued, "I'm guessing you're an American, sir." Taking his hand, "And it is Evan, Charles. Yes, I am from Michigan. Nice to meet you sir," as I looked down at this diminutive man, who couldn't stand more than 5' 3" tall, if that with his golf shoes on. "And I'm Penelope, Evan," came the greeting from Mrs. W, who had to be a good 6" shorter than her husband.

Standing as though he was guarding Buckingham Palace, the equally trim, Mr. Abernathy, arm pointing to the right, stated, "The Tee awaits you all. Have a wonderful day, as long as it lasts." Not comprehending what he said, other than to enjoy ourselves, we pulled our trolleys down the crushed gravel path towards the modest green tee box, not measuring more than 5 yards square, with another box, of similar size, awaiting Penelope, some 25 yards ahead of where Charles and I would hit first.

"How long a stay for you in England, Evan?"

Charles asked as he bent over to tee up his ball, then looked up at me as he took a couple of practice swings. He added, "'Tis the only thing missing from Broome Park; a good driving range to warm up with a few swings."

"My wife and I have been here 38 days, with two to go, before we head home." I replied. "Forty days!" came the exclamation from both Charles and Penelope. "Please tell us what you've seen thus far and tell me your wife's' name also." Penelope inquired.

After hitting our balls, and then Penelope's, I explained, smiling to Penelope, "Lisa and I spent 8 days in Scotland, another 8 in Leeds and the mid-country, and the balance around London and the Southern half of England. We spent last night in a Bed & Breakfast, overlooking the Dover Cliffs." "Oh, they are marvelous, aren't they?" came Charles' response. After Mrs. W's drive, Mr. W continued our conversation, "Evan, my lad, if I may be so bold as to ask, please tell me what you do for a living that allows you to spend 40 days on Holiday with your wife?" "Not at all." I replied and continued," I had a Seat on the Mercantile Exchange, Chicago Board of Trade, for 20+ years, and sold it about 10 years ago, to pursue some less stressful endeavors." "Trading what commodities?" Charles asked. "Originally, I traded currency, on the New York Exchange, when I was employed, by another company, and then, I got myself into trading Corn Futures, and the Good Lord blessed us fairly well, which has allowed us to do other things." I tried to humbly explain.

"Well done, Lad. That's quite a success story. I'm a retired Banker myself, having been with Barclays in London for the last half of my career, but, nothing as exciting as the pressure of arbitrage." Charles knowingly acknowledged what my job pressures must have been like, over the years. "Well, today, we'll leave the memories of employment behind us and have ourselves a wonderful round of golf." He encouraged.

"Well hit, Mrs. W." Charles yelled as Penelope hit her second shot towards the first green.

The next few holes passed quickly as Charles, truly a humorous man, kept me laughing so much, I really wasn't paying much attention to my golf, and I was 3 over par, after three holes. Walking up to the Par 3 fourth hole, Charles held Penelope's cart, stating, "You promised Lovey, that you'd hit from the back tees here today," said

Charles as he pointed and explained to me, "The tees over there, are only 75 yards from the hole and you don't have to go over the pond, we have to when playing here." "Come on Lovey, it's a mere 110 yards from here and besides you birdied this yesterday."

Looking at me and smiling with pride, knowing I now knew she had birdied this hole, she scowled at Charles, "Never an advantage you give me Charlie, I'll just have to do it again from here today". "You see Mr. Christian, what competitiveness does to 47 years of marriage. Just for spite, she probably will birdie it again," said Charles as we reached the tee box and began to extract our clubs of choice for this short Par 3, with the last 50 yards of flight over a small pond.

Then, as Penelope turned back to her bag and cart to select a different club to hit, she stared back towards the Clubhouse a not so distant mile or so South, she looked at us in despair and pointed towards the sky, saying, "Looks like our round for today is over Gentlemen!" "Oh no! Charles cried. "You're right Lovey. It looks as though we will have enough time to get back before it engulfs us. Well Evan my lad, it is up to you, but Mrs. W and I have seen this before, and it was predicted that this might happen today, and if you desire to keep playing, you may find it a bit hard to see."

As I focused back at the Clubhouse, not very further South, I could see a dark gray mass rolling toward us. It was similar to what I had witnessed from our Bed & Breakfast room early this morning, while overlooking the Channel. Charles then continued, "Like I said Evan, it is up to you, as I know this is your only chance to play Broome Park, but it will get like pea soup out here in about 20 minutes." Not knowing quite what to do, but knowing any delays would prevent me from getting in all 18 holes, and figuring it couldn't be all that bad, and that I could find continue playing by looking at the hole by hole map on the back of my scorecard, I replied to them both, "I think I will try to continue playing, as my wife is expecting me at 5:00PM and I won't be able to finish if I wait and come put to play later. Perhaps I can play fast and if I lose a ball here and there, that's ok. Thanks, but I will give it a try. It has been a true pleasure meeting you both," I said, as I reached out to shake Mr. W's hand. "Are you sure you want to do this Evan?" Penelope asked and continued, "You may not be able to see very far." Smiling back at them, I again thanked them, as they began to pull their trolleys behind them, walking away from me. Then Charles stopped and said, "Just in case, there are shelters every few holes if you need one, and the first one is adjacent to the 5th Green. If it gets bad, you can hold up there for a while, and who knows, it may break quickly, and you'll be able to play fast after that. Good luck Lad." They walked away with a quick pace and looked back and waved a couple of times.

CHAPTER 2

MAKING A BIG MISTAKE

Watching them a few more moments, I turned to focus at the task on hand, which was to hit near the Flag and make birdie myself and play the remaining holes in a couple of hours, tops!

After a couple of practice swings, I hit a smooth wedge right at the pin and was happy to see it land and stay on the green, guessing it was about 6-7' from the hole. Alright! Let's have some fun, as I replaced my club in the bag, and looked one more time at the Witherington's, who just happened to make one last stop to look back at me and wave. Off I went.

It was even closer than I thought, just inside 5 feet, with about no break at all, so I confidently removed the flag, laying it near the hole, spent a quick glance at the line, a couple of practice strokes and voila, Birdie! Simultaneously, reaching my bag and looking towards the Clubhouse, I saw Charles and Penelope still hustling South, and then, looked above Broome Park, to the ominous gray sky, which was getting closer by the minute.

Teeing up on number 5, this Par 5, was definitely reachable, especially with the Southern tailwind, which I was now just noticing. My Callaway driver, hit the Slazenger squarely and even before the ball landed, I was off walking towards it, smiling and thinking maybe two birds in a row, or perhaps even an eagle. Reaching my drive of about 315 yards, I now surmised I was less than 200 yards from the middle of the green, which was where the flag appeared to be located, so as I turned to my bag to pull out my 5 iron, I glanced back South, and froze for a brief moment, as I watched the Clubhouse, disappear like a wave coming on shore, completely washing over a small pebble. Broome Park was gone, out of sight in an instant, and the gray rolling mass, was no longer in the sky, but right at ground level, coming towards me at a speed faster than Charles and Penelope's walking pace back to the building.

Knowing I had made a mistake not to join them in walking back, but buoyed by my drive and the chance at back to back birdies, I took a quick practice swing, exhaled and launched a perfect shot, which was on a beeline to the flagstick. "All right!" I said out loud, acting as my own gallery and cheering section. However, looking back as I walked quickly North, the morning fog, which had been over the channel some 7 hours ago, was now making its' statement over Broome Park's wonderful acreage.

As I approached close range to the green, I could see my ball was about 10' from the Cup and a possible eagle 3, but that exhilaration, was short lived, as my backwards glance, now saw the fairway of the 5th hole, begin to disappear. Still, the task at hand was the putt and I took just a bit longer to ensure the right line, stepped up, stroked and watched the ball disappear in the cup. With a slight fist pump for my efforts I bent over, retrieving my ball, place the pin back in the cup and by the time I got to my trolley, the fog was beginning to set upon me.

"Oh boy Evan, what have you done?" I said to myself, as a bit of panic set in, and as I remembered what Charles had said about the Shelter near the

5th green, I looked in all directions, and located the shelter to the West of the Green about 75 yards away. That too, looked like the fog was beginning to cover it. Now running full tilt with the bag and trolley, in a wild ride behind my right hand, I got about two-thirds of the way there, when EVERYTHING disappeared. I stopped in my tracks. The Shelter in front of me was gone, as were the trees behind and to its' right. Looking back at the green, I saw nothing, and within seconds, I could not see my bag and trolley, which were less than 3 feet from me.

Like a blind beggar, I reached out towards my trolley and hit it with my outstretched hand, which was also beyond my sight. Good Lord Evan!

I now had no choice but to try and find the Shelter. I turned and gained my bearings and begin the step by step walk, in what I hoped was the correct direction. The 30 or so steps took me a good two minutes, as I couldn't remember what the ground looked like between the green and the shelter, so I had no idea if any depressions in the landscape lie ahead of me. Then, just as I heard and felt a gravel sound beneath my feet, my trolley was pulled from my hand. Stopping to reach back for it, I pushed it back and pulled again, and it bumped something, as I snagged it forward. What the heck was that, a fallen branch, a stump? Then, as I turned back to gain my bearings, I took one more step forward only to hit my shin on something. Reaching down, I felt a bench. I was inside the shelter and had hit the shelter's bench, which I could not see just 3 feet below my eyes.

I grabbed for the bench again, and sat down in relief that, at least, I had found the shelter. I pulled by trolley towards me, as though it was a security blanket, and I was the frightened child scared of the dark. However, it wasn't dark, but all gray. I put my hand in front of my eyes and slowly moved it away and before I could completely out stretch my arm, my hand disappeared! No wonder ships crash in the fog. Then I recalled Charles' comment, "As thick as pea soup." This was beyond anything I could imagine. I looked up and pondered the inside height of this shelter, as from 75 yards away, it appeared to be no higher on the outside than 15 feet, so inside the vaulted ceiling between the 4 posts would be just shy of that height. The fog prevented me from even seeing the ceiling.

As I sat there, I soon realized three things; First, my heart rate was rapid from all the anxiety of finding cover, and I also found that my clothes were mildly damp and I was getting cold. Not since the 1967 Masters, had the famous line by Roberto Divicenzo, seemed more appropriate; "What a Stupid, I am!" His was for not correctly reviewing and then signing his final round scorecard, which would have won him that Tournament. My stupidity was for not listening to the Witheringtons, and my fate might be somewhat different than losing a tournament.

At any rate, I was somewhat sheltered for the moment, as I thought, so now what do I do? After a few moments, I thought, Lisa! I need to first call Lisa, to inform her of my predicament. I turned my trolley around to gain access to the golf bag pocket in which I placed my wallet, car keys and, as I reached around inside, my cell phone. And then, after I call Lisa, I will call the Broome Park Pro Shop, to let them know where I am. While dialing Lisa, I took the scorecard from my back pocket, to find the Club's phone number on it. I was so concerned with that, that I failed to notice that there was no dial tone when I tried Lisa. There was no noise from touching the phone keypad and nothing from the earphone, dial tone or otherwise. It was a dead phone and it wasn't working. I tried dialing the Clubhouse as perhaps the distance to Canterbury was affecting my cell phone's ability. Again, no dial tone, no ring, no sound at all. What the heck is going on here?

Now what do I do. No communication, no visibility and I was getting colder by the minute. I was sure that Charles and Penelope would have informed Olivia inside the pro shop, but what could they do? To be certain, they knew I was stuck out here for a while. Perhaps they would get an electric golf cart and slowly drive it out on the course, through holes number 1, 2, 3, 4 and 5. Charles saw me as I left number 4 green, just before the fog engulfed the Clubhouse about the time they arrived back there. He must have told them that he told me of the shelter near #5. They would place 2 and 2 together and assume I was held up right here.

That's it. It would only be a little while before they would be here. What do I do until they come get me? I was truly getting cold, and at the beginning of the round, I was thinking the walk would warm me, so I left my light jacket in the car and was only wearing a golf shirt and sweater. Looking around, I was still baffled by the density of the fog. Sitting on the bench in the shelter, I could just make out the gravel beneath my feet, but out of curiosity, I walk slowly towards where I expected one of the 4 shelter posts to be located. Reaching out like a blind man, my right hand eventually hit the 4" by 4" wooden post, and as I stood on my tiptoes and reached as high as I could, I just barely touched the bottom of the Shelters' roof shingles, guessing the overhanging roof, was about 8 ½ feet above the ground.

It was then that I first heard some voices in the distance. "Lawrence, do you see them yet?" Came the question from the first voice heard. "Not yet Eddie. They should land in about two minutes" was the reply from Lawrence.

"Hello" I yelled, hoping they would hear me. "Is anyone there? Where are you guys?" came my second inquiry. Nothing but dead silence followed. "Eddie, they are going to have a difficult time with the fog beginning to come in", was the comment from Lawrence. "They have dealt with landings like this before, they should have no problems." Retorted Eddie.

Truly, these guys sounded like they were less than 50 feet away from me, so once again I called out, "Hello anyone; Lawrence? Eddie? Can anybody hear me?" Again, no reply came my way. This is ridiculous as I walked towards their voices, I encountered a dip in the terrain, almost losing my balance. "Hello?" as once again I called out. A few steps later, I had made it to the 5th fairway. I knelt down, touching the closely mown grass, and began walking across the fairway, guessing it would take me 25-30 steps before reaching the right rough.

As I got to about the middle of the fairway, I made one last plea for help; but to no avail as no comments came back to me, although I could still hear them talking to each other.

"Here they come Eddie. He's coming in too low." Cried Lawrence. It was then, that I heard the engines of what sounded like a prop plane, and suddenly, I realized their conversation was about airplanes that were about to land. "Up you bastard, get your nose up!" cried Eddie. Their voices were coming from my right, while the engine sound was getting louder and coming in from above left. "Up, get it up Captain!" They both cried out. Then the sound and wind thrust of an airplane came roaring right by me, as I dove to the ground fearing it was coming too close to me.

Then, I heard the brief squeal of the tires hitting the ground, or runway or the fairway. Whatever, the plane had landed, and now I could hear the running steps of Lawrence and Eddie, as they chased the plane down crying, "Dear God no!" It was then I heard the explosion and felt a burst of heat from that direction followed by the sound of trucks coming from my left, as though they were driving right down the middle of #5 fairway.

"What the heck is going on here?" was my only verbal response. Then as quickly as the voices and sounds of planes and trucks had come upon me, there was once again, nothing but silence. One last try. "Hello? Anyone?" Nothing.

NO sounds, no voices, no planes, not even any wind noise. I again checked my cell phone but it was still not working. Now what do I do?...

Somehow, I needed to make my way back to the house. I can visually remember most of the first 5 holes, so I kept my left shoe in the right rough and my right shoe in the fairway and walked in the direction of Broome Park. Before long, I reached the end of the fairway, or should I say, the beginning. I recall a center grass cut section, so I walked more to the middle of the fairway, and there it was; A 3 foot-wide mown section of grass that steered me towards the 5th tee boxes. In a few steps, I found where Mrs. C would have teed off, and a little further South, where 30 minutes ago, I hit my 300 plus yard tee shot, in the other direction.

Now I had to negotiate #4 Green, the Pond guarding its' front and the tee box, all within a 135 yards of each other. I managed to do that without falling into the water and found the tee box, and moments later the 3rd Green. Thank goodness the holes were essentially boring and straight, as I found #3 fairway, its' tee box, then the 2nd hole and finally the first fairway and Tee. Just as I began looking for the Clubhouse Building all of a sudden, the fog began lifting and I could see the Starters' Booth, but with no sign of Mr. Abernathy.

As quickly as the fog had covered everything, it was now lifting, and there, less than 100 feet from me, Broome Park, appeared in all its' glory.

I had made it back in what seemed like 45 to 60 minutes or so. Rats. I had left my watch inside the golf bag on the trolley, inside the Shelter near #5, and I never bothered checking the time my whole trip back to #1 tee.

"Mr. Christian! Are you alright Mr. Christian?" Came the concerned question from Olivia as she exited the Pro Shop door, running towards me, with an anxious face. As she neared me, again she said, "Are you alright Sir? You had us worried. The Witherington's told us you decided to play on. We should have told you in advance of the anticipated fog. Mr. Abernathy mentioned he said, "Have a wonderful day, as long as it lasts.", but perhaps that didn't register with you?" Olivia asked.

"He did. I remember that now, that he did say that, but I thought nothing of it until you mentioned it." I stated.

Olivia then stated, "You must be cold from being out there 2 hours." We tried to find you. We sent our Greenskeeper, Mr. Dunston, and his golf cart out to #5 Shelter, but when he got there, he found nothing but your trolley and bag", as Olivia pointed to a golf cart that had my rental bag on its' back.

"Wait a minute. You say someone came out to get me?" I asked. "Yes, sir, Henry Dunston, our Superintendent." She replied. Just then, another person, a tall, well dressed, gentleman came out the same door as Olivia had, and walked towards us, as by now we were almost at the Pro Shop entrance.

"Mr. Christian, Sir. I'm David Stellars, the Club Manager. We are truly sorry for what happened. Are you OK?" He asked.

"Yes, but I am very puzzled. Olivia said your Mr. Dunston drove a cart out to get me. Which way did he come?" I asked.

Because this has happened before, we instructed him, to drive down the right side of every fairway and the left side of every green, because for holes #1 thru #5, the Tee Boxes are situated immediately to the adjacent left of the previous green, so in thinking you might come back that way, as others have done, we hoped Mr. Dunston would run into you that way." Mr. Stellars explained.

"But I did come back that way. As you say, I did find the shelter near #5, and when I began hearing voices, I left the shelter and forgot about my bag and trolley, and tried yelling at those voices, but they didn't hear me." I said as we entered the Pro Shop.

"The dickens you say." Came the question from the smallish, weathered looking man.

"Mr. Christian, this is Mr. Dunston, our Course Superintendent." As David Stellars steered me towards Henry.

"Are ye ok lad? I found your clubs and yelled as loud as I could in all directions, but ne're heard a sound back." Said Henry.

"This doesn't make any sense to me. I stayed maybe 10 minutes at the Shelter, and then, I did hear voices, two of your employees perhaps, a Lawrence and an Eddie? I asked.

With an equally puzzled look on his face, Dunston replied, "'tis sorry I am, Mr. Christian, but we have no workers with those names at Broome Park, inside or outside of the building. Which way did you walk back to the Clubhouse?"

"That's just it. Mr. Stellars told me the way you came out to get me." I started to explain. But before I could say more, Henry replied, "Correct you are sir, we always drive our rescue carts on the right side of fairways 1 thru 5."

"You couldn't have, because that is the way I returned to the Clubhouse, only I didn't take 2 hours as Olivia said, I swear it took only 50-60 minutes at most. I only stopped when I heard the plane crash." I stated.

"Mr. Christian, it may have seemed like only an hour, but please take a look at the clock over there," pointing to the wall clock above the Pro Shop counter, Mr. Dunston continued, "You see, your tee off time was 11:00 and Mr. Witherington estimated you had played the first 5 holes in about 45 minutes, more or less, so add the 60 minutes you say it took to get back here, that would make it 13:00 or as you say, 1:00PM." Again, Henry pointed at the clock, which read, 3:00PM. "And, what was that you said about an airplane crash?" He inquired.

It was then, that I felt like I was somewhere in the Twilight Zone, and not wanting to make them think I was totally crazy, I told them a little white lie, and said, "Perhaps it was something crashing in the distance, maybe on the M8 Highway."

"Maybe so, if anyone was trying to drive during this fog, they would likely chance an accident. Maybe we should check it out, Mr. David." Said Henry, looking towards Mr. Stellars, who nodded in agreement, as he turned towards me, and said, "Well, you're here with us now, Mr.

Christian, let us get you some dry clothing to put on, as you must have a chill from being out there 4 hours......" With his last word tailing off, as though he wished he had not said it.

"Thank you," I said gratefully, "That would be nice, but actually I do have some clothes in my car, into which I can change, if you will point me towards the Men's Locker Room."

Mr. Stellars pointed to the left of the Pro Shop counter and said, "Down the stairs to the left, is our exercise room with lockers just prior to entering that room."

A bewildered "thank you" came out of my mouth, as I walked out the door and then seeing Mr. Dunston ready to drive the cart away, I called out, Henry, "Before you take it away, sir, I left my watch and car keys in the bag. How dumb of me?" I stated while reaching in the bags lower compartment. "Here they are. Thank goodness I didn't lose those. I'd really be in a fix then. Thank you for trying to rescue me Henry. I'm sorry to have made such a dumb decision as to have stayed out there, when the Witheringtons advise me not to do so."

"You're alright now laddie. It's only cost you 4 hours of your time, that's all." He chimed back at me. "Have a good day sir."

"Hold it a second Mr. Dunston, you really came after me soon after Mr. & Mrs. Witherington got back into the clubhouse?" I asked.

"Yes sir, I'd say about 10 minutes tops after they called my walkie-talkie phone, which couldn't have been 5 minutes on top of the ten." He stated. "Then, it was slow going, but I was out at #5 Shelter no more than 10-15 minutes later. I truly called for you for several minutes, before I guessed you tried coming back to the Clubhouse via a different route, instead of the way I came out to get ye." He smiled. "But no matter, yer' OK now Mr. C. and none the worst for ware. Glad I am that yer' fine lad." As he walked to his cart and drove away.

Standing there by myself, I looked towards the Pro Shop window, seeing Olivia retreating from where she was viewing my conversation with Henry. With no one else outside, save Henry and his cart, I walked over to my Rental Car and took some clothes out of my suitcase, and walked slowly back into the Clubhouse, pausing once more, to look again to the North, where whatever had happened, surely didn't make sense to me at this moment.

CHAPTER 3

CALLING LISA

After removing my damp clothes and putting on another pair of pants and one of the three sweaters I brought with me, I warmed quickly and placed the used shirt and pants in the plastic bag given me by Mr. Stellars. Looking around the smallish locker room, I saw the sign for the exercise room and swimming pool, so I strode down the short hallway and looked through the glass windows into a room filled with a total of 12 elliptical machines, treadmills and stationery bikes combined. It was typical of any nice resort in the States, except that the walls were painted concrete, a sign that the owners wanted to preserve as much of Broome Parks' internal feeling as possible. Walking further, I opened a heavy wooden door which let me admire a swimming pool of about 50 feet in length and only 3 lanes wide; a sure sign this resort catered to adults who may want to stay in shape via swimming, rather than American Hotel Pools, whose larger sized pools, were meant for accompanying children to enjoy. It then struck me that I had not seen any children at all, during my first stroll through the resort. This was truly a get-a-way for adults. Still, as I walked out of the pool area, I was amazed that this 400 year-old edifice, which certainly did not contain an indoor swimming pool in the 1600's, had made it adjust to the desires of the 21st century tourist.

Speaking of adults, I needed to call Lisa as it was now about 3:15pm, so as I climbed the stairs to the Pro Shop and walked out to my car to store my clothes, I wondered what was I going to say about this to Lisa? Although I might have a hard time convincing the Broome Park Staff of my experience, surely Lisa would believe me, but that for me, was not going to be enough. Why did this happen, was the question that needed to be answered.

So, walking back into the building, I thanked Olivia again, and asked where Mr. Stellar's office was located. Coming from around behind the counter, Olivia, with all the customer service of the best Ritz Hotel anywhere accompanied me through the dining area and to the Main Offices of the complex.

Knocking on the open door's entrance, Olivia stated, "Mr. Christian was wondering if he could talk with you a bit sir." David stood up and again greeted my hand saying, "Absolutely, Mr. Christian, please come in." "Thank you, Olivia," was said by both of us simultaneously. "Are you a bit warmer now sir?" He inquired.

Sitting down in response to his out-stretched hand, offering me to do so, I replied, "Yes, thank you again for your consideration. I was wondering if you might have a vacant room for tonight and possibly even tomorrow night as well?"

"Why yes sir, are you thinking of trying to play again tomorrow, as the weather might be a bit better, all though I should tell you sir, that the forecast is for another round of late morning fog, so if you decide to play again, we would encourage an early tee time which I would be happy to arrange for you." He asked.

"Actually, I just thought of staying and walking around the grounds with my wife, who is sightseeing up in Canterbury as we speak. I am planning to go get her and come back in time for dinner, so if you will tell me where I register for a room for two, I will stop bothering you so you can get back to your work." I replied.

Standing up and leading the way to check it, he said, "You are my work sir, and let's make sure you and your wife, get a room for one or maybe two nights." Down across the front entrance, where I had wandered before golfing, was the registration desk, with a Miss Knightly staring at the both of us as we approached.

David introduced us by saying, "Miss Knightly this is Mr. Christian, our guest who got caught out on the course today, and he would like a room for he and his wife for tonight and possibly tomorrow as well. Mr. Christian, this is Katherine Knightly, our Room Clerk."

Looking at me with a compassionate expression, she exclaimed, "A pleasure to meet you sir, and we are all glad you made it in safely. We are all so sorry for the scary experience you must have had out there. It has happened a few times before in my 3 years here at Broome Park, so let us see if we can't make up the bad experience for you, by giving you and Mrs. Christian our 3rd Floor, corner room, which looks South and East towards our beautiful gardens. When tomorrow's sun rises, there is no prettier view in all of Broome Park."

"Why thank you that would be fine" I responded as I gave her my credit card and passport. I was truly impressed with the incredible hospitality exhibited by the entire staff, even despite their obvious concern for my "lost on the course" encounter. I thanked Katherine and David and told them I would be back from Canterbury in about an hour or so and would have dinner at that time. They made my dinner reservation and off I went to my car, calling Lisa as soon as I exited the building.

"Evan," came the first comment from Lisa, "How was your round of golf?" Again, she was always first concerned for me. I replied, "Oh it was very interesting dear, how was your day in Canterbury?"

With her usual enthusiasm, she said, "Well, I'm just about to go into the Museum here, because there is a special hour long tour, so I'm glad you called, so that if you came back early, you aren't waiting for me. I should be at the pick-up spot, just about 5:00PM. Is that good for you honey?"

"Sure Lisa'" I replied, as I stood by my car in

the parking lot, "However, I was wondering,….. Honey, I know this may sound crazy but I want us to stay here at Broome Park tonight. I can call the Inn we reserved there on my drive to you, cancel our room and we can make it back here in an hour and a half or so and have a delightful dinner. Would that be alright with you?" I begged liked a little boy asking for a new toy.

"If that is what you want to do Evan, I'm good with it. I would be happy to see Broome Park. Uncle Patrick must have been right about something, wasn't he?" as she agreed with my plan and made the assumption of why we were staying there. Boy oh boy, was she going to be shocked when I tell her about the airplane crash and all.

Explaining my plan, I said, "Thanks Honey, I'll leave here in about 20 minutes or so, as it may take a few minutes more to get there if the Fog hasn't totally lifted on the M8."

Lisa abruptly asked. "Yes, I heard from some shop owners here, that the fog was particularly thick further South. Did it affect your golf game at all?"

"A little," was my reply, not wanting to begin my explanation of the strange occurrence just yet.

"Anyways, I'll see you in about an hour honey, enjoy the Museum. I love you," were my closing comments. Lisa's sweetly replied to me was, "Love you to."

Standing there in the parking lot, I felt a bit sheepish, feeling as if I had told a little white lie, but I wanted to be face to face with her when I begin my dissertation of the days' events, so it made sense to me to wait. After hanging up with Lisa, I stood and gazed North towards the distant, fifth fairway, imagining the flight path of the plane, which must have come from directly over the house, as the whole of the contour of the land, from the house to #5 Green and beyond, was as virtually straight as a runway. Following the line back to the building and further South, my gaze in that direction, reflected a similar straight line view from the front of the property line, some ½ mile or so, up to Broome Park Mansion itself, as I imagined, what the property might have looked like, minus a golf course. The house would have made a perfect signal tower of any incoming planes, to guide them in towards the eventual touch down. Reviewing the land made my experience have more logical sense than ever. Just what did happen today, I simply had to find out. At least I was glad Lisa didn't object to staying here tonight.

I gazed up at the 3rd floor, Southeast corner room, which Miss Knightly so politely suggested for our stay. Would there be any more clues in that room? What would it look like in the morning, looking South and East? Thinking that, I gazed towards the gardens that she mentioned would look so pretty if the morning sunlight favored us tomorrow.

Reflecting on all that happened, I opened my car trunk, to look inside my briefcase to get the number of the Canterbury Inn to cancel our room for the next two nights. Shutting the trunk door after dialing, I then sat in the drivers' seat to make the call. Remarkably, I wasn't the least bit upset with the 100lb. cancellation fee, with this late a no show, but I didn't care, I had to find out more about what happened to me today, and staying on site was the only sure way I could find out why?

Now, I was only 25 minutes away from Canterbury and Lisa wouldn't be ready to be picked up for at least another half hour, so I had some time to kill, and rather than go back into the building, I exited the car, and began walking slowly to the gardens, and their focal point, a botanical building, I assumed. This one story, rectangular long edifice, had only a central door, for its' front access, with multiple vertical windows to the right and left of the main entrance, about every 5 feet or so. The windows had white panes, making the building look more along the lines of American Colonial Architecture than that of a 17th century mansion, so I assumed this garden building had been added years after the house had been built. Still, it was a beautifully simple building, with gardens on all the 3 sides which I could see from this view, so I decided to walk down and see what was around back of the building. I took the right side route and as I walked the 75 feet or so to the right end of that building, I took more notice of the other, larger garden building, which looked more in design, like Broome Park itself, with 3 arches, supported by pillars of stone, evenly spread in distance, giving it the look of the Roman Coliseum's archways. Beautiful flowers and hedges surrounded all of these buildings, making it look like Alice in Wonderland's Garden Maze. Lisa was going to love walking these grounds tomorrow, but for now, for some reason, I had to see behind this rectangular building.

As I reached the end of the building, I noticed that the fog had thickened again. It was nothing like earlier today, but if this fog was on the M8, my drive to Canterbury, might take a little longer. As I turned the corner of the building, around back, I saw part of a small pond, about 150' in width, or roughly the same width, as the building. I say I saw "part of the pond", because fog had already enveloped the length of the pond. In other words, I couldn't see across the pond, to know exactly how long it was. So, I decide to walk around the right side of it, and see for myself, the actual size of the pond.

After about 30 feet of walking, keeping myself about 15 feet or so, from the ponds' edge, the fog virtually dropped over me again, much like it had on the 5th Fairway earlier. I could barely see the edge of the pond, so I stopped, thinking I had better return to the parking lot and go get Lisa.

As I turned to trace my steps back to the building, I heard voices coming from the middle of the pond. However, this time, the voices, sounded like those of young children, and along with hearing them talking, I heard water splashing as well. I stopped so as to not make any noise as the voices and splashing continued.

"Hello?" I cried out towards the center of the pond. "Is everyone OK out there?" Why I had chosen those words, I have no idea, but if there were children in the pond, I didn't want them to be frightened by someone they didn't know. "Hello? Can anyone hear me?" As I found myself repeating the 5th fairway scenario, I suddenly realized, it was happening again.

No one was going to hear me, just like with Lawrence and Eddie; Someone was out there talking, but there was no way, they could hear me. I decided to try and get a closer look, as I thought, with the pond and the children playing in it, perhaps they would be close to the edge of the pond, so if I got close enough, who knows what I might encounter. I turned around again and proceeded to walk around the pond. My estimates were that the pond was almost oval in shape, with its' length being about the same as its' width, because after about a hundred steps, the edge of the pond, began to curve to the left, so I followed it, even though I could barely see a yard or so of water after the ponds' edge.

However, the children's voices were getting louder, as I got closer to them. One last time, I cried out, "Hello? Is everyone in the water

OK?" .... After pausing, I heard no sounds for a couple of seconds, and then, ...the continuance of the children's playing, laughing and splashing again filled my ears. But no one responded to my call. Just like before, I was within yards of these kids, and about the same from Lawrence and Eddie and the plane!!! Still, no sightings or contacts were made here.

As I was about to continue walking closer to the ponds' edge, the fog began lifting, almost as fast as it had dropped on the pond and around me, and like, airplane pilots that begin to see clouds dissipate and clear skies emerge, the fog was breaking into little sections, or evaporating or both, until, in about 15-20 seconds, the entire pond emerged from its' gray covering, sitting there in quiet stillness, with not a ripple upon its' surface.

The Garden Building also came into view, and beyond it, the top of Broome Park was visible over the top of the closer building. The pond ended up being that almost perfect oval shape, I had guessed it would be, and the structure of the garden building width, almost perfectly matched the width of the pond. Whoever had designed that building meant for it to obscure Broome Park's view of the pond. Perhaps it was because, two or three hundred years ago, maybe the pond was for bathing? Who knows? All I know is that I heard children's voices, just like I heard the plane land right by me. I was now more determined than ever to find out what happened, and how it happened. The couple hundred yards back to my car went quickly, as I hopped in and made my way to the M8 and Canterbury, and Lisa. What would she really think of my story?

CHAPTER 4

DINNER WITH THE WITHERINGTON'S

During the 5 minutes it took me from Broome Park's parking lot, to the M8, the fog completely lifted, so the drive to Canterbury took the expected 25 minutes, and right on cue, as I turned on the main street to look for Lisa, she was crossing the street to our assigned meeting spot. She saw me and waved after reaching the curb, just as I brought my car to a stop, right in front of her.

After sitting down in the car, she leaned over and gave me a kiss, as I was pulling back into traffic, which wasn't much as I would have expected at 5 o'clock, but perhaps we weren't in the business section of Canterbury.

"OK, big boy, what is the real reason you want

me to see Broome Park?" Lisa asked with a huge smile, as she continued, "What is it that Uncle Patrick wanted you to do or see there?"

Not wanting to scare her or even make her laugh at my story, I thought for a second, before realizing the only way I could have this make sense, was so see if it might happen to the both of us, if the fog came in the next morning, like it had today, so my reply to her was simply, "The place is fantastic. The golf course wasn't much, but I still fun, although I couldn't play a full 18 holes, as the fog came in so thick, we had to quit playing."

Interrupting me, she said, "Who is We?"

"Oh, I played with a delightful retired couple from London, The Witherington's. Charles and Penelope, and together, I don't think they stand 10 feet tall, but he was so funny, that I didn't even care that I played lousy." I said, trying to think of what I might say next to Lisa. "But, again, the course is not the main attraction at Broome Park. It is the main building. Honey, externally, it hasn't changed since it was built in the mid 1600's, and the surrounding grounds, have the most beautiful gardens you could imagine. It's nothing specific that I want you to see, but just the whole experience."

"Well, great, I'm looking forward to being there. Actually, Canterbury was nice, but it would have been more fun with you there, so seeing more of Broome Park together, will be great for you and me." She retorted.

Continuing my explanation to her, "I can't wait to see our room, the Manager, David Stellars and his Room Clerk, a Miss Knightley,…"

Interrupting me again, Lisa said, "Oh, you met Kiera Knightly now, did you?"

"Actually, I think her name is Katherine, but she assigned us, what she described as the 3rd Floor Room, with the best Morning View, as it is situated so we can see East and South at sunrise, for what Miss Knightly states is the prettiest view of their magnificent gardens." I said pragmatically, trying to diffuse any jealousy from Lisa. "Anyways, the Lobby, the lounge, the dining hall, the whole place is incredible, and I just wanted you to experience it with me. We have dinner reservations in about 40 minutes, so…"

"I'm in Evan." She said, smiling once again. I always love seeing her smile.

The drive went quickly as we exited the highway, making our way towards the property. As we approached the entrance and got within eye view of Broome Park, Lisa remarked, "Wow, this is nice. And you say this building was built in the mid-1600's. It looks in as good shape as any Arlington property built after World War I."

"It's funny you say that, because Uncle Patrick said the Estate was used by........the Royal Canadian Air Force, as their Headquarters, during World War II." And as soon as those words come out of my mouth, I suddenly questioned myself, "Could my 5th Fairway encounter today have anything to do with the War?" Nonsense; I don't and never have believed in the supernatural or telepathic, but as I drove our car to the Front Entrance for Check-In, I couldn't deny what I had heard this morning.

As we excited the vehicle and walked toward the Door, Lisa exclaimed, "Evan, this place is unbelievable. Thanks for talking me into coming here." Well, at least that hurdle had been cleared. Now it was How and When to explain the story to her which was my next obstacle.

"Mr. Christian!" Came the welcome from Katherine Knightly, "And to you Mrs. Christian, as well. We're so glad you decided to stay with us. Here is your room key and dinner is in about

25 minutes, so you can freshen up a little before then."

"Miss Knightly. My wife Lisa." Was all that I could think of saying at that moment.

"Why of course, Lisa. I understand you were in Canterbury today. How was the experience for you?" came the friendliest of questions, from this friendliest of hotel clerks.

"It was fine. Thank you for asking." Replied Lisa, as we took the Key and followed Katherine to the staircase. "After the first landing, turn right, and go down to the end of the Hall, and up those stairs, which stop directly in front of your room. We apologize for no elevator, but the Oxenden's didn't know of them 400 years ago, and the new owners in 1995 wanted to keep the same atmosphere. I hope you are OK with climbing the stairs. I will have Edward our Valet follow with your bags." She explained as she waved for the young man, in his military looking outfit who sprang into duty.

"Yes, that's fine. They really didn't change a whole lot of the home when they converted it into the Hotel/Condo, did they?" I retorted.

"Wait until you see your room. It is one of the rooms, that is most "untouched" during the renovations, as you might imagine it when the Baronetcy still owned the home prior to the 1920's", when it fell out of the family's possession", explained Katherine as she walked up the first flight of stairs with us, and then, bid us adieu and returned down to her office.

"The service here is quite nice," I said to Edward, as he walked in front of us towards our room. "That's kind of you to say, sir. We are all put through very special training to try and make our Guests as welcomed and comfortable as possible during their stay. Let me take you Key Sir," as he opened our Door, letting us walk through first.

I could see Lisa's reaction to this beautiful room, being one again, with at least 16-foot ceilings. The crown molding had to be 12" in depth, and the coloring in the room was surprisingly attractive. But why shouldn't it be, as the lobby, the restaurant, Mr. Stellars' office, the Foyer and everything about this place was incredible. And the service was beyond extraordinaire, as they were treating us as though we were part of the Oxenden Family. "Why shouldn't they!" I thought. We are a part, albeit a very distant part, nonetheless, of the original and longest running tenants of Broome Park. "Thank you, Edward." I said handing him a five pound note, rather than a couple of quid. Somehow it seemed appropriate to be more generous.

As Edward shut the door behind him, I turned to a wonderful kiss from my wonderful wife, "Evan, thank you again. Just look at this room, and this view. Oh look, the Gardens; How pretty. I wonder what's around back of that long building?" As she pointed to the same one I walked around less than an hour or so ago. "No, you don't," was my internal response to her question!

"Let's take a walk before dinner, I want to see the gardens before it gets dark." She asked.

So rather than hang up our clothes, we were back down the stairs in two minutes with just our sweaters to warm us in the evening air. Miss Knightly smiled and waved, as we walked by her, as she was attending to new guests at check in. "She wants to walk the Gardens a little before dinner." I said as I motioned to Katherine as we exited the front door.

Once outside the front door, I stood there looking South as the land gently sloped away from the House, and admiring the Trees that guarded that property line, it was truly breath taking.

More than a half mile of green grass, with none of it being part of the golf course, lay between us and the grove of trees that looked fairly thick was something to behold. Off to the right was a single row of trees that separated this first view from the Southwest part of the Golf Course. The sky was still cloudy, but the fog had finally lifted from the entire landscape, but standing on the white gravel front driveway, I imagined Horse and Carriages from days gone by making their way up the slope to meet the Baronet and His Family. I then found myself wanting tomorrow to be thick with fog, if only to see what might happen??

"Come on Evan," yelled Lisa, as she was already 100 feet towards the left gardens. I quickly caught up with her as she was gently holding some of the longer flowers that beckoned to be touched. "What must life have been like here 400 years ago, when this was first built?" She quietly asked us both, as she meandered around the waist high hedges that separated different parts of this garden. From the front of the building, we walked around it, just like I had 90 minutes ago, until the pond came into view again.

"Oh, my goodness!" She cried, "You wouldn't imagine this pond being here, when we were on the buildings' other side. How lovely it is. The water looks very clean. It must be spring fed. Are there any other lakes or ponds on the golf course?" As she turned towards me.

"As a matter of fact, yes." I said, "I know of one for certain." As I smiled thinking of my walk back from the shelter. As we walked around the pond, to about the spot I was when the fog lifted right after I heard the children's laughing and splashing, almost right on cue, Lisa said, "I can just imagine the children who lived here, coming down to this pond, to cool off and swim on warm summer days." How right you are, I thought as I again relived in memory the sounds of earlier.

By the time we strolled around the pond and came back on the North side of garden building, the Sun peaked out underneath the gray clouds in the low, South West sky. "It must be marvelous on full sunny days", Lisa said, as we walked towards to House. I don't know why I was thinking House, but after our walk around the grounds, it felt more like home than ever.

Reaching the East side of the building, Olivia was walking out of the Pro Shop, locking it up for the day, as evidently no golfers bothered to go out again, once the fog had lifted. "Mr. Christian!"

She said, as she reached out to greet Lisa. "I heard you were bringing back your wife to stay with us. We're so glad you did. Mrs. Christian, my name is Olivia, and I work in the Golf Pro Shop. We were so worried about your husband this afternoon. But we were so glad when he made it back safely from the course. Have a great evening and we will see you tomorrow, as she walked away, beyond the guest parking lot, to evidently the Employees parking lot, beyond a row of trees."

"Quietly turning and smiling ear to ear," Lisa inquired, "And, what was that all about? Don't tell me you got lost on the course. I thought you said you played with the Wimpoles or something?"

Sheepishly, I tried to explain, "Well first of all, it was the Witherington's that I began playing with, but then, the fog rolled in, and they, and I'm afraid to say, everyone else on the course, went back to the Clubhouse, when…" Interrupting me, Lisa said, "So, you stayed out there and lost your way." Rolling her eyes, she said, "Smart Evan. Very smart. I can see the headlines back home, 'American golfer drowns while trying to get in a few more holes!' Smart. Very smart."

"Come on in dear. I will explain what happened over dinner." I said as we walked back in the front entrance, thru the lobby and into the dining area.

"Evan my boy!" Came the cry from the table by the front window. It was the Witherington's. Getting up and coming over to greet me, Charles shook my hand and said, "We must have been up in our room, when you returned from the course, and before we came down. The staff told us you were going to Canterbury to get your wife. How lovely, you are my dear." Said Charles as he greeted Lisa, and right behind him Penelope uttered, "Lisa, my dear. We were so worried for your Evan." She said shaking a finger at me like a Mother admonishing her little boy, "We told him, to come back in with us when the fog rolled in, but just like all men…."

Charles blurted out, "Please join us for dinner, we want to hear from you Evan, just what you did during the 3 ½ - 4 hours you were out there alone."

"Oh yes my dear, I'm Penelope," Penelope reinforced the invitation, as she guided Lisa to their table. "I said to Charles just as we got back to the house as the fog dropped, Evan will have a difficult time getting back here. But to tell you the truth, the same thing happened to us the very first year we played here, so we can't be too critical of Evan." She smiled as she motioned us both to sit down and join them.

Now grinning ear to ear and beyond, Lisa looked at me as she said, "Yes Penelope, I too want to hear all the details of this afternoon. Let's do have a nice dinner together."

Feeling like Superman's X-ray eyes were penetrating my very being, Lisa's stare was only noticeable and felt by me. Having to explain the details of today's events in front of others, was not what I had planned on doing, when I wanted Lisa to come to Broome Park. However, perhaps Charles and Penelope would add a little levity to dinner and maybe the true explanation would come later tonight.

Penelope continued the conversion with, "Lisa, Evan told us you have 3 almost Grown Children. Please tell me their names Dear."

Reaching into her purse, and retrieving her latest pictures, Lisa handed them to Mrs. W, saying, "Alex is our 20 year-old son, while Deidra and Sheryl are our 18 and 16 Year old Daughters. Alex is entering his 3rd year at North Park College in Chicago, and Deidra will be a Freshman at the University of Michigan, while Cheryl will be starting her 3rd Year of High School."

"Oh, my dear, such beautiful children, but then why shouldn't they be, as you and Evan are such a handsome couple." Penelope exclaimed as she handed the pictures to Charles.

"Does the boy play golf as well, Evan," said Mr. W. as he glanced at the photos and passed them over the table back to Lisa."

"Alex plays whatever is in season and has a love for Cross Country running but his biggest love is fishing. As we speak, he is probably with my Father, fishing a river in Michigan." was my response.

"Fly fishing!" exclaimed Charles, "One of my true loves. If you had more time Evan, my lad, I would tell you to go back North to Scotland and fish the many streams that feed Loch Lomond. Actually, any of the streams of Scotland will provide the avid fisherman with a lifetime of pleasure. You will have to return with your Son."

The wait staff came and got our drink orders while Lisa, wanting to be cordial to Penelope, took the brief lull in the conversation to ask, "And you and Mr. W., what about your family?"

"We've just one son, Steven, who lives in Zurich

with his Swiss wife, Natasha and their daughter, Petra, who will be 19 next summer and will enter University next fall. Like Charles, Steven is in banking and very busy. We get to see them during the Holidays and once a year we visit them in Zurich, but it is so difficult to have your family away from you. So, we keep ourselves busy with charitable activities and playing golf whenever we can. We have been coming to Broome Park since the investment group owners bought the property in the mid 1990's and turned the property into a Golf Course and kept the charm intact in this lovely home. Isn't it magnificent?" Penelope insisted.

Lisa quickly responded, "Oh my yes. Evan and I just walked through the Gardens and they are so beautiful. And our room on the 3rd floor is so charming. We were going to stay at the Canterbury Inn tonight but Evan called me after," turning to give me a glance, "his experience today and I'm looking forward to seeing more of this place."

"So, Evan we hate to remind you that we suggested you come back with us, once the fog rolled in but never mind that. Tell us what you think of our English Fog?" asked Charles.

Turning to me to join in the inquiry, Lisa smiled and added, "Yes, Evan, what was it like?"

"Well, ah ha," as I cleared my throat and tried to think of how to start. First off, thank you Charles and Penelope for warning me. I'm only sorry I didn't listen to you…"

"No apologies needed. We must tell you, the first year we played here back in 1997, the same thing happened to us. Luckily the fog lifted after an hour and we met Mr. Dunston, coming out to get us, as we returned but Olivia in the Pro Shop told us you were out there 4 hours?" Charles exclaimed with sympathy to my predicament. "4 Hours. You must have been freezing!" He added.

Chiming in, Lisa reiterated, "You were out there, alone in the fog, for 4 hours?" Then turning to Penelope, she added, "He also goes fishing well after midnight, in areas where Bears are known to live. My Husband, the Sportsman!"

"Don't be too hard on him dear. We Golfers often make more mistakes in our decisions, than we do with our golf swings and as Charles said, it happened to us as well." Penelope said, trying to lessen my embarrassment.

"Thank you, Penelope." I continued, "You are all correct. It's just that now Lisa will have something on me, that she can always bring up when she wants to question my decisions on anything else." I said, smiling at Lisa.

The small talk continued through drinks and dinner, and I was able to dodge any specifics about my experience as we discussed the English Stock Market, Southern Great Britain's sites, we had evidently missed and a myriad of other items, not related to Broome Park.

However, early in the conversation, Charles had mentioned something that didn't go further, due to Penelope insisting Charles let my encounter alone as we talked about other things. Now reflecting on what he had said earlier, about, "I too know a little about Broome Park's History prior to Lord Kitchner becoming the Owner," was his passing comment 40 minutes before. So as dinner ended and the four of us casually made our way up the stairs to our rooms with Penelope and Lisa several steps ahead of us, Charles leaned towards me and to my surprise whispered, "Did 'ye hear anything when you were out there today?"

Turning my head towards Charles, I came to a halt, half way up the staircase and seeing this mischievous smile emanating from Mr.

Witherington, I frankly didn't know what to say but ended up quietly blurting out, "It has happened to you too?

Not saying a word, Charles simply nodded his head and took the next steps, each rather more slowly than the others, so as to distance the girls from us, so we could talk more. "It is obvious that you have not had a chance to tell your lovely wife about what happened today, but let me assure you, it was real."

My eyes and ears riveted on Charles, he continued, "The first time for me was when I came out here the first year it opened with some Banker friends of mine and I did exactly what you did when the fog rolled in. They all went back in and I continued. At that time, we were on the back nine, about the 11th hole, which is fairly close to the Clubhouse. They went back in but I continued and found shelter, just like you did, only on #13 tee box, where I hear all sorts of things."

"Like airplanes landing and crashing?" I offered.

"Airplanes? Heavens no. I heard carriages and footmen." Charles retorted.

"Carriages and Footmen?" I pondered.

71

"Yes, and when one of them said, "Almost home now Sir Henry"." Charles continued with the enthusiasm of a Father telling his children a bedtime story, "But the voices ended as quickly as they had begun. I yelled and yelled for someone to hear me but to no avail."

"Yes, yes." I insisted, "That is exactly what happened to me, except that I heard and felt, the heat from the flames of an airplane crashing. I swear."

"Evan my lad. I truly believe ye'," Charles insisted. "I do. The trick is; will Lisa?"

From down the 2nd floor hallway where Penelope and Lisa were standing came, "Come on you two, Lisa and I'm sure you too Evan, are both very tired from this long day. Come on Charles, stop with your stories and let them get to their room", chimed Mrs. W. as she opened her door, turning to hug Lisa, wishing her a good night. By the time we got to them, Penelope turned to me with a similar hug, pulling me down to here 4' 9" level, and quietly whispered in my ear, "Think carefully Evan, how you tell the story to Lisa."

Smiling at me, as I straightened up, she winked at me and Charles, who was smiling in agreement with whatever he thought Mrs. W. had said to me, he suspected it was about today's events. Charles hugged Lisa, and the two disappeared behind their closing door, making me think how Broome Park had disappeared in the fog much earlier. Grabbing Lisa's arm and beginning our ascent to the 3rd floor, Lisa stopped, turned to me, and demanded, "Evan David Christian! What happened today?"

Not saying a word, but continuing up the stairs, I opened the door, kissed her cheek as she preceded me into our Broome Park abode and then closed the door behind me.

CHAPTER 5

BELIEVE IT OR NOT

The 10 seconds of silence seemed like a millennium but eventually I had to turn around and be confronted. However, I waited and walked over to the corner window of our bedroom and looked towards the Garden Building and beyond, where the night sky didn't quite allow me to see the pond behind it. Looking West towards the already disappeared August Sun, there was still a slight sliver of light coming from the horizon, underneath the clouds. Then, feeling Lisa's eyes piercing the back of my head, I turned my gaze South, towards Dover, and began my explanation to her;

"Do you remember this morning at 5am?" I began my exclamation, as I turned to see her standing frozen in the room hallway. As she shook her head, half yes, half no, she replied, "What has this morning got to do with what happened here today?"

I sat down in the wildly patterned wing chair, next to the window, and invited her to sit next to me, in its' twin chair, on the other side of the small round table, which had a few magazines on it. She slowly walked towards me, gently anchoring herself to the chair, while I looked towards the ceiling in hopes of opening with the right words.

"The sky over the channel this morning, had the thickest of gray clouds I have ever seen. They were hanging over the water, not far from its' surface, almost giving the appearance that the waves crashing on the Dover Cliff shores, were being generated by the clouds themselves, as though they were being spun underneath them and thrown to the shore." I paused. She started to speak, but I held up my hand, signaling I had more to say.

"Those especially thick clouds, were in fact, heavy fog, sitting offshore, waiting for a favoring wind to push them on land; which they did about 2 hours after we left Dover after breakfast, and about 45 minutes after I started playing golf with Charles and Penelope, the fog reached

Broome Park. Evidently, the Witherington's had experienced such a fog several years ago when they first came here and that experience made them immediately depart back to the Clubhouse." I stated as I was trying to get the courage to move on to the "experience" of today.

"I've already heard that you continued playing and that they came to get you on the course and the fog kept you from seeing your rescuer, but you made it safely back." She said in a somewhat impatience manner. "Then what?"

"Lisa, the Greens Superintendent here is a Mr. Dunston. He was the guy who drove out to near the 5th green, on exactly the same path on which I came back to the Clubhouse. "I continued. "I mean exactly! When I asked him that route, he described it in detail, and I know I came back via that route."

"So, you missed each other in the fog by a few feet." She responded.

"No. Let me explain. When I asked him the timetable of my being lost, Mr. Dunston and the rest of the Staff here confirmed it was almost 4 hours that I was gone. I calculated every movement I made from when the fog first engulfed me, until I got within 100 feet of this building, which is when the fog finally lifted. And my timetable had a 2 hour gap from theirs. Two hours! And we didn't come near each other on the route out and back from the clubhouse, because I was 80 years away from him." I stated as I firmly stared at Lisa's eyes, letting her know I wasn't lying.

"What do you mean 80 years? She stared back.

"There is the shelter near the 5th green. The fog was so thick, I could not see the interior roof of the shed, while inside of it. I couldn't see my outstretched hand. I couldn't see the ground on which I was standing." I exclaimed.

"I get it. The fog was thick." She smiled.

"No, you don't. Not yet anyways." I continued. "After I had sat there for a few minutes, I then got out my cell phone and attempted to call you first, and then, the Pro Shop, all to no avail as my phone was not working. After a few more minutes of waiting, I began to hear two voices. Two male voices; a Lawrence and an Eddie. I called out to them several times, but to no avail. I walked out of the shelter towards where the voices emanated and several more times yelled out to them. I heard every word they were saying, but they never heard me."

She was now fixated on my every word.

"What's more, is that they began seeing a plane approach them from the South and I heard the plane as well. Not a jet, or little Piper Cub type plane but a World War II Bomber Plane, coming to land on the 5th, 6th and 7th fairways of the Broome Park Golf Course. I heard the plane come in, touch down and crash land, complete with an invisible fire ball of flame but a fire ball that generated heat that I did feel. A truck then rushed by me towards the burning plane. Of course, I didn't see that either, but I heard it go by only a few feet from where I was standing. And no sooner than having heard all of this, everything became silent again."

"So, you're saying you were transported back 80 years to World War II and you heard all this but saw nothing?" Looking intently in my eyes, she then began to laugh. "Honey, I am sorry, I do believe you heard something but...come on Evan."

"Lisa, I probably would laugh as well but listen to this." I continued. "Thirty minutes before leaving here to pick you up in Canterbury, I took a walk behind that Building," pointing out the window, towards the garden, "And I heard the voices of children playing and splashing in the pond. The fog had set back down for a few minutes, covering 99% of the pond. I did see the edge of the pond, and I walked around it towards the voices, yelling again, Is anyone there?"

"Evan!" Was her one-word reply.

"Ok. How about this. On the way upstairs after dinner, as Charles was explaining his fog experience from 15 years ago, right here at Broome Park, he whispered to me, "Did you hear voices out there Evan?" I said yes and then remained quiet.

"Both of you now think Broome Park is haunted?" She smiled trying not to laugh. "I believe you. Did Charles hear planes and children as well?"

"No. He said he heard carriages and a footman saying, "We're nearly home Sir Henry", I exclaimed.

"So now we're back in what century?" She smiled again, only this time, not holding back her laughter.

"Go ahead and laugh Lisa." I said, as I rose from my chair, going over to give her forehead a kiss, "But if the fog comes in tomorrow, you and I my dear, are going for a walk in it."

The rest of the night, before finally falling

asleep, we talked about Uncle Pat and his desire to want me to see Broome Park, somehow, trying to make a connection with him, through today's experience. Meanwhile, Lisa was fascinated with the rooms' décor and commented, "I wonder whose room this was 172 years ago?" Which, of course, was the year Aunt Elizabeth Phoebe Tanner, married Sir Henry Chudleigh Oxenden, the 8th Baronet of Broome Park Baronetcy.

CHAPTER 6

BREAKFAST WITH THE WITHERINGTONS

The morning arrived with sunshine coming through our window, just as Katherine Knightly had hoped for us. Lisa was already up, having made herself some hot tea in our rooms' kitchenette. She was sitting in the corner window chair, reading one of the magazines within reach. "Good morning Sir Evan. I hope your Lordship slept well?" She smiled as I sat up in bed, trying to right myself. At least she was correct about one thing, I had slept well. "Shall you be riding to the hounds today or do you have to receive Sir Benedict from London?" She continued to tease.

"Ok, smarty pants. What do you want to do first this morning?" I asked.

"We can start with asking Charles what else he heard during His encounter." She said.

"Oh, so you do believe me now?" I retorted.

"Well, having spent a restless night, while you slept, I reflected that in 25 years of marriage, you have yet to lie to me, so something definitely happened to you out on the course and if what you told me about Charles' encounter, then let's just say, my curiosity wants to investigate this thing further." She smiled as I got out of bed, walked over and hugged her.

"I will shower as quickly as I can." I replied. "I am guessing Charles and Penelope will already be down at breakfast. We can continue our conversations then."

Ten minutes later, we were down the stairway towards the dining hall and saw the Witheringtons, just receiving their oatmeal as we walked in.

"Come Christians, please join us. We have only just had our morning Tea and now our porridge has arrived." The diminutive Charles stated, while standing to greet us. "Slept well I trust?"

"Good morning Lisa", was Penelope's greeting

as Lisa sat next to her, each hugging one another. "Come have some Tea with us. They have many to choose from. Charles and I have enjoyed Earl Grey for years. Do you have a favorite?"

"Earl Grey sounds perfect, thank you Penelope." Came Lisa's reply. "And how did you sleep last night?"

"Always delightful my dear. As long as I fall asleep first, I don't hear the wounded rhino next to me and I don't wake until first light, so I have been up for a couple of hours and am already on my 3rd cup of tea." Penelope informed me, while poking at Charles' ribs during her teasing lament.

"Tis true Lisa, I must confess, I am surprised you didn't call the front desk to complain of my nocturnal sounds, if you had heard them from one floor up. Deviated septum, my Doctor says, will always make me a noisy sleeper, I'm afraid. But my dear wife is immune to the noise after many years of marriage, so now I just bother those in adjacent rooms." Charles chuckled, as we all did with his honest explanation.

"But the real question is, how did Master Evan fare for the night?" Charles inquired.

"Actually Charles, I slept like a baby. After the rather long and interesting yesterday, I needed a sound sleep." I replied. "And I got it, thank you. What's good for breakfast?"

After ordering, eating and polite chatter that helped Lisa get to know the Witheringtons better, Lisa could wait no longer and waited until she had Charles staring at her and then she looked directly into his eyes, saying, "Mr. Witherington,"

"Not so formal my dear, please Charles." He replied.

"Charles." She self-corrected, "After hearing Evan's explanation of yesterday, he added you experienced something similar. Is that correct? And how long ago?" As Lisa's inquisition continued.

"Oh my. You'll have me telling things I have yet to share with Penelope but since you've inquired and it is relevant to Evan's experience, I have no choice but to share what happened to me 8 years ago." Charles talked as we all moved our chairs closer to the table, including Penelope, as she smiled in anticipation of Charles narration.

"It was mid-August, like now, and Penelope and I had played nine holes but she had slightly sprained her ankle on a depression in #9 fairway and decided to go in, while telling me to play the back nine by myself. The Pro Shop had warned of impending heavy afternoon fog, so most play had been completed by noon, so, like Evan, I had the course to myself. As I reached #13, I noticed the fog drifting in from the South and saw the players on the adjacent 17th fairway walking at a feverish pace to try and complete their rounds before the fog settled. We had played in fog the day before, but it was more that we couldn't see our balls more than 100 yards away, rather than the pea soup Evan saw. So, I continued thinking the same would happen that day. By the time I reached 13 green, the furthest point West on the property, the fog had blocked everything from my vision to the East. The fairway, the Clubhouse, and even the trees I had just chipped out of to get on the green." Charles paused….

Then I chimed in, "That's exactly what happened to me on #5 yesterday."

"I know, we should have forced the issue with you to come back to the Clubhouse with us." Penelope offered.

"I thought the same my dear," said Charles, "but, something inside me wondered if you Evan, might not end up hearing sounds and voices like I had."

Lisa blurted out, "What do you mean sounds and voices?"

"Well my dear," Charles continued, "at the 14th Tee Box, there is a shelter just like the one Evan found near #5, so I took temporary refuge in it. Right behind the tee box, there are some hedges covering the wooden fencing, which serves as the property line. Just outside the fence there is dirt road, which t-bones into the dirt road that follows the Western border of Broome Park. As I sat in the shelter, the fog became so thick, I could barely see the hedges, just 10 feet away from me, and just when I started thinking about how long the fog would last and how was I going to get back to the Clubhouse, I starting hearing the sound of horses and a carriage. Then, coming from the direction of the t-bone intersection just right of the shelter about 50 feet or so, I heard the carriage and horses come to a stop, I assumed, preparing for a right or left turn. I stood up and walked toward the hedges, which had all but disappeared in the fog, but I wanted to get as close as possible to the road over the fence but that too was invisible to me.

As the horses' feet were shuffling on the dirt road, I then heard the hoofs of one horse and that is when I heard a man's voice, saying, "We're almost home now, Sir Henry." Then, I heard that single horse, and another, and then the horses of the carriage and carriage itself, begin to turn South right towards me. That is when I yelled, "Hello out there on the road, can you hear me?" Neither the horses, nor the carriages slowed down, even as I yelled a second and third time. They just continued South until I couldn't hear them anymore."

Penelope chimed in, "Well how did you know that it wasn't a local horse and carriage?"

"Penelope love," Charles challenged, "When was the last time you saw, except the kind for Tourists in Regent's Park London, a horse and carriage of any kind? And besides, what person would call another Sir Henry, especially 100km from London? You know very well that we investigated the history of Broome Park and there were several Sir Henry's who lived here in the past 400 years."

"You know of the Broome Park Oxendens?" I interrupted.

Looking at me as though I were a ghost, Charles was silent for a few moments before saying, "How do you know of the Oxenden Family?"

Smiling back at both Witherington's, I

began, "You remember during our first few holes yesterday, when you asked, "Of all the courses in England, why did you choose to visit Broome Park?" As they nodded, I continued, "Remember me saying my Uncle Patrick wanted me to visit here?"

"Why yes." Said Penelope.

"My Mother and my Uncle Pat's last name is Tanner, and after researching some family heritage, they discovered that their Great, Great, Great Grandfather, James Tanner, had a daughter, Elizabeth Phoebe, who married Sir Henry Chudleigh Oxenden, the 8th Baronet of Broome Park."

Smiling ear to ear, Charles said, "Well I'll be a blue nosed baboon. Your Uncle wanted you to discover all you could about Broome Park. Is your Uncle still alive?"

"Unfortunately, no. He and Aunt Marnie came on a vacation to Europe several years ago and they disappeared without a trace. The last we heard about them, was that they were traveling in the mountains of Switzerland, but that was 5 years ago." I said with a lump in my throat.

"Oh Evan," said Penelope. "You, poor lad; not

to have known what happened to them. We are so sorry for your both."

"That's kind of you Penelope," I said, "So after they were declared dead, we thought we owed it to him, to come where he wanted us to visit; Broome Park."

"And you say, your Uncle Patrick never visited here?" exclaimed Penelope.

"While his research taught him a great deal about Broome Park and the Oxenden's, as far as I know, he never came here." I said.

"It's clear to me then, that during your Uncle's research, he must have discovered or read about the Haunting of Broome Park." Charles retorted.

"What do you mean, Haunting?" Lisa asked.

"After my experience in 2015, I went back to London and did some research and found articles about Ghosts and Spirits all over Canterbury and County Kent." Charles began.

"I've heard of the fictional stories of the Ghost of Canterbury, but you're not saying that throughout County Kent, other spirits come back to haunt people today?" I inquired.

"Why not? Something happened to you yesterday and something happened to me 5 years ago and to the Mayfield's just last year." Charles explained.

"Who are the Mayfield's?" I asked.

Leaning forward on his forearms, upon the table, Charles had a different look on his face as his began to describe more about Broome Park than I could ever have imagined. "Yes, like meeting you, our encounter with Henry and Deidra Mayfield started with a round of golf, on a weekend just like this one; Warm and windy, with afternoon fog. The difference between then and the fog of yesterday, is that it "hung" over Broome Park."

"What do you mean hung?" I asked.

"Yesterday, when we first saw the fog coming North, it looked like a large wave coming ashore, engulfing everything in its' path, right?" Charles stated. I nodded. "Well the fog that day with the Mayfields, seemed to hover, like a tall ceiling over the grounds. It barely touched the 4th floor towers, yet it was every bit as dark grey as you experienced. However, as we looked to the East, West and North, we could still see in the distance, perhaps 2 miles in each direction, light from the sun, reflecting on the ground, all around Broome Park on 3 sides. It had been sunny since daybreak, but this was about 3 in the afternoon. Moreover, the fog stayed that way, and didn't move further North or recede any bit South for the next 2 hours, which is what it took for us to complete our round of golf."

Penelope, Lisa and I sat motionless waiting for his next statement.

"I was just happy to keep playing and after a hole or two, paid no attention to the big grey blanket less than 100 feet over my head. Even when one of my wedge shots went high enough to disappear in the clouds, and came down, like a drop of water from a faucet, right on to the green. I smiled at Henry", who said;

"You're lucky Charles, once the clouds caught my ball and didn't return it to earth." Of course, I presumed he was jesting, and I continued walking to the green, but when I made my birdie putt, Henry commented, "Well, the Ghosts of Broome Park are certainly generous today."

I turned and smiled at him as I retrieved my ball from the cup. Then, I noticed his stare, and said, "What do you mean, generous?"

"It is funny Charles," said Henry, "You inquire about the Ghosts generosity, but not about the Ghosts."

"I said nothing. The girls had gone on to

the next tee box, but Henry and I lingered a bit and slowly walked to #12, waiting for more explanation from Mr. Mayfield."

"Charles my friend," started Henry. "Why do you think the Tales of Canterbury have captivated our country and those who visit County Kent for Centuries?

"It is probably because some people like a good ghost story every once in a while." Charles offered. "It's good for the tourism, I suspect as well. What's your opinion?"

"County Kent has had ghost stories for hundreds of years. Scientists have studied them. People have testified to having seen apparitions. These are ghost stories that, for many, are valid, real and true!" Henry smiled as we reached the tee box.

"Well, then I thank the Ghosts of Broome Park, for returning my ball, or should I say, place my ball on the last green, close enough for me to enjoy a rare birdie!" I exclaimed, not wanting to challenge my playing partner.

"Laugh all you want Charles, but they are real. I have seen them as well." Henry continued.

"Oh Henry," Deidra retorted, "You're not

boring Mr. WItherington with your Ghost stories, are you?"

As Charles took a second from his dissertation, to sip a cup of coffee, Lisa brought us back to reality for a second, as she interjected, "Well, I like your story Charles, because, our eldest daughter is named Deidra, so I just like hearing stories that involve that name."

All this time, I had sat silently, listening to Charles' every word, and then I too interjected a comment, "The Mayfield's didn't happen to say where they lived?"

Penelope, obviously the voice of memory of such meaningless details, contributed her comments to our discussion, "Why yes, as Deidra and I walked along that day, she mentioned that her family had lived in Brighton for generations. Why do you ask Evan?"

My heart froze as I began to remember more of the details from Uncle Pat's lineage, and for that matter, my lineage. I recalled that my Grandpa Tanner was born in Brighton, and that the Tanner Family had been there for generations as well, and sometime in the late 1800's, one of the Tanners, married a woman named, Deidra Taylor.

"Penelope, Mrs. Mayfield didn't happen to mention her maiden name; did she?" I inquired.

"Why as a matter of fact, she did. What was it now?" She said, suddenly energized about the discussion. "Deidra? Deidra? …….. Deidra Taylor Mayfield!" She exclaimed with pride.

"Evan, what are you getting at?" said Lisa.

"My Mother's Grandfather, Charles Harry Tanner, was the 6th Son and 7th Child of Frederick Tanner and Frederick married a Deidra Taylor." I quietly said to us all.

"Well, what do you know," exclaimed Charles. "You're a blood relative to Deidra Mayfield."

"Maybe, just maybe" I said. "I'm sure there are plenty of Taylors in Sussex County England, and we're talking about a time frame of 130 years back to make the blood connection."

"Evan, it's quite clear to me. After Henry Mayfield explained to me the numerous paranormal encounters over the years in Canterbury and other parts of County Kent, and with what Henry, and I, and now you, Mr. Evan Christian, have experienced, your family is reaching out to you from bygone times," cheered Charles.

Trying not to be theatrical or too serious, but

not knowing how else to state the fact, I quietly stated, "Grandpa Tanner's, Grandmother, was Deidra Taylor of Brighton, England."

For what was more than a few moments, all four of us sat motionless, around our dining table, in the lovely estate at Broome Park, which suddenly, took on an entirely new meaning for me.

Breaking the silence, Charles smiled, patted my shoulder, and said, "I would have liked to have met your Uncle Patrick, Evan. He certainly must have known something about Broome Park, to have insisted you visit here."

Not wanting to let go of possibly more Broome Park information, I looked at both Charles and Penelope and asked, "What else did the Mayfield's say?"

Charles smiled and turned towards Penelope and said, "You see my dear, I'm not crazy like you thought." Then, turning back towards me, he continued, "The funny thing about the Mayfield's, is that they wrote it off as some type of hallucination. You see, Henry told me, that every once in a while, they indulge themselves in marijuana, which they were doing the first time they heard voices inside of Broome Park."

Marijuana or not, all the information was

almost too much to comprehend, as I sat there, looking at Lisa, who, like always, was smiling back at me. However, a feeling of serenity came over me, as I pondered the possibilities of what meeting the Mayfield's might bring. Turning my eyes towards Charles and Penelope, it was as if they were waiting for me to make the next move in this paranormal game of chess. All I could come up with was, "Well, it certainly gives us a lot to think about, doesn't it?"

All four of us burst into mild laughter, as the breakfast tension eased. Penelope broke the momentary silence with, "If you would like Evan, I wrote down the Mayfield's address and phone number in my address book, which is up in our room, and I would guess the Mayfield's wouldn't object if they got a call or a visit from you. Would you like for me to get it?"

"Penelope, that would be very kind of you." I responded.

"I'll be just a few minutes." She advised as she stood up and walked towards the exit.

Charles re-starting the conversation said, "It is about 1 hour and 10 minutes from here to Brighton by automobile Evan. What are your thoughts?"

"Precisely what I was about to ask of you Charles. Thanks for anticipating it." I replied. Then, turning to Lisa, I asked, "What would you think of delaying our return home for a few more days. Dear?"

"Having come this far, I guess it makes sense to find out as much as we can, while we're here," came her answer. "Besides, we had talked about trying to get to Brighton during our trip anyways, so why not Evan. Let's do it!"

"Here it is!" announced Penelope, talking loud enough for the entire dining room to hear, as she returned from upstairs. "She said for years they lived on Duncan Street NW, but they recently moved, I think in the last year or two, to Abernathy Street. Yes, here it is, 122 West Abernathy. So, I would say about an hours' drive and a bit more to get there from Broome Park." She smiled looking up from her address book, to seeing all of us smiling back. "Oh, this is so exciting. Will you please take my card, and make sure, whatever you discover, or not, that you call us prior to your returning to the States?"

Lisa, reaching out to hold Mrs. Witherington's hands said, "Oh Penelope, you are so kind to be concerned and wanting to help. We will for sure call you either way." Then, turning towards me, "Well, Mr. Christian, it appears, we are off to County Sussex?"

Trying to be practical and thinking about driving all that way, without knowing if the Mayfield's would even be there, I asked one thing more of the Witheringtons, "Charles do you think you could call Mr. Mayfield, first to see if they are even home, and secondly, to pave the way for our coming over there, as they might be tied up with other commitments or maybe not even be there in the first place."

"Evan lad. You're a man after my own heart, as I was thinking the same things." He replied. "I would be happy to call Henry and Deidra, share a bit of our discussions with them, to see if they might have interest in talking with further with you. Sound acceptable?"

"Perfect!" Came the joint reply from Lisa and I.

CHAPTER 7

OFF TO BRIGHTON

Following Charles into Broome Park's Parlor, we sat and listened to Charles' phone call with Henry Mayfield, which we could tell from his reaction, was working out as planned.

"That's great Henry. I will tell the Christians to call your number upon their arrival into Brighton around Noon. After pausing to listen, what's that Hotel name?... Barrister House. Good. We will let them know and they can tell you upon reaching you. Thanks ever so Henry. Regards to Deidra. Bye now." Smiling as he gently turned off his cell phone, he turned to us and said, "They can hardly wait to meet and talk with you. They have some errands this morning, for which they were just leaving, so we caught them at a perfect time, as they have nothing else planned for the afternoon and they would love to meet some possible distant relatives, or fellow ghost chasers.

"Oh Charles," blurted Penelope, "He didn't a'tall say such things."

"On my word, my dear. Those were the precise words from Henry and Deidra, as they were on the telephone together." Charles retorted. "Well, Evan and Lisa Christian, it appears your trip will be leading you to County Sussex and the Beach Town of Brighton. Don't forget to take in the Brighton Pavillion, as it is one of England's more famous oceanfront buildings. Fascinating Moorish architecture from the mid-1800's, and Brighton is a wonderfully quaint town to begin with, so we know you'll enjoy your visit there, whether or not your Heritage Search, is successful."

Our quick goodbyes to the Witheringtons, with promises to call them, were followed by a quick conversation with David Stellars of Broome Park, to let him know of our change in plans, but that we might return from Brighton later anyways, but will call to let them know.

Packing our bags and taking one last look around our Room and outside, Lisa gazed Southward noticing the darkening skies. "Evan;

do you think our drive to Brighton, will miss the incoming fog?"

"Yes, not if we go quickly." I said, as I picked up both our garment bags and Lisa grabbed both our duffel tote bags, and walked out the door and down the stairs to return our key to Miss Knightley.

"Here is the map Mr. Stellars suggested you might need for your drive to Sussex. Though your mobile GPS may guide you even better, but the map does point our interesting things along the way. We certainly enjoyed having you stay with us Mr. & Mrs. Christian. We hope you come back soon to stay again." Responded Miss Knightley, just as Mr. Stellars was exiting his office, having overheard our goodbyes to Katherine.

"Yes, do come again. We'd be happy to serve you once more. Safe travels and good luck." As David signaled to the valet to take our bags to the car, he shook my hand and Lisa's as off we went through the front door, following our bags.

Once in the car, Lisa served as Co-Pilot and Navigator for our short journey to County Sussex and Brighton. Along the way, we watched as the fog held off going further North, and possibly blanketing Broome Park once again. I somehow wanted that to happen, while we would be on the grounds. We would encounter that scenario soon enough. For now, it was off to make Family Connections; we hoped.

CHAPTER 7-A

MY MOTHER'S AND UNCLE'S ROOTS;

Brighton, England

For years I had heard family comments about the birthplace of my Maternal Grandfather. Grandma Tanner had made a journey there, long after Grandpa Tanner had passed. My folks too, had made their way down to Brighton, on a trip to London, and even my cousins, Uncle Patrick's two youngest daughters, Kaitlin and Karolyn, visited there during a European trip, which had started in London, with a day trip to "discover their roots."

In retrospect, I had regretted, that Lisa and I had not planned on going to Brighton on our 40 days in the UK, but now we were solving that issue, by chasing another; The Mayfield's, and their possible link to the Tanner Family, by way of the Taylor's of Brighton. More importantly, for their, or more correctly, Mr. Mayfield's surreal experience at Broome Park, which warranted further investigation on my part.

Was Charles Witherington's account of Henry Mayfield's encounter with the distant past an accurate interpretation? Heck, I had first doubted Charles' own story of overhearing Sir Henry Chudleigh's groom informing the 8th Baronet that Broome Park was nearing, even knowing what I had gone through myself. Still, the phone call between Charles and Mr. Mayfield indicated the Henry's interest in talking with a possible descendant and blood relative of his wife.

So, as the sign welcomed us to the Town of Brighton, I felt my pulse begin to quicken in anticipation of meeting Henry and Deidra (Taylor) Mayfield. Following Lisa's GPS navigation, we soon found ourselves on Abernathy Street, and then the block after London Street, in front of 122 West Abernathy and the quaint, and charming, small English Tudor home, covered with Ivy.

"Evan," began Lisa, "I must confess this whole thing left me skeptical, but coming her to meet Mrs. Deidra Mayfield, and her possible 6th generation connection to our own Deidra, gives me goose bumps."

"Me too", I countered. "Let's go see what we can find", as we closed our car doors and began focusing on the front door of 122.

The buzzing of the doorbell caught me off guard, as I had expected an American, "Ding-Dong" chime, forgetting we were not in Kansas anymore. As the door opened, the opposite stature of the diminutive Charles Witherington, took up most of the entry door opening. Henry Mayfield was 6'5 and 270 pounds if he was an inch and a pound, and his English Tweed sport coat, vest and bland silk tie, gave a typical British look from this gentleman from Brighton.

"Hello, you must be the Christian's," came Henry's welcome. "Please, come in our humble abode."

After letting Lisa enter first, my outstretched hand was greeted by an immense right hand similar to an NFL lineman's paw. "Mr. Mayfield, first thank you for agreeing to see us. I....", I began but was quickly interrupted, "Please, call me Henry and 'tis no interruption." He replied. "Enter the Mayfield home."

"Thank you." Came from both Lisa and I simultaneously, as we stepped through the narrow foyer and then left, into a living area about 20' x 15' with a picture window taking up most of the South wall, letting those inside have a clear view of West Abernathy Street. Two "flower patterned" wings chairs flanked sides of the picture window, with a round table and lamp adorning the view. The opposite wall was filled with pictures galore of everything from family to buildings to outdoor scenes, the entire 20 feet in length. A large 4 cushion couch sat underneath the pictures, while a half dozen assorted pillows, lined the back of each cushion, inviting anyone to sit and position the pillows to ones' liking, which is just what we did at Henry's request, while he walked to the west end of the room, and yelled to his wife, "The Christian's are here my dear!" Turning back towards us, he commented, "She's in her sewing room, as usual, stitching up some thing or another. Can I get you anything to drink?

"Water would be fine", said Lisa, probably feeling a little dryness in her throat in anticipation of this meeting, while I said, "The same for me would be fine as well, thank you."

"Give me a minute and I'll be back with

the water but make 'yerselves comfortable and look closely at any pictures that may raise your curiosity."

As we waited, both of us were fascinated with the number of pictures hanging on all 4 walls. The west wall of the room was dominated by the 4' x 4' fireplace opening, with porcelain tiles adorning the sides and top of the opening, with a flat fieldstone hearth, which stood out 18" from the fireplace. Fresh, unburned logs were in the grate, ready to warm the room at a moments' notice, with several inches of ashes all around the inside of the fireplace indicating that, even in the warmth of this August, the Mayfield's used their fireplace frequently. The picture above the fireplace was a wonderful replication of their home, complete with flowers in bloom, hinting that the artist drew the painting in the springtime. Either side of that picture, were several other 12' x 12' paintings and sketches, all vertically lined to form a rectangular horseshoe around the fireplace. A small bookshelf was situated behind the right wingchair and the corner wall. More pictures surrounded the picture window on both sides and the 12" of space between the top of the window and the crown molding of the ceiling.

The East wall was half in size of the West wall, due to the foyer entrance, but that too, had a dozen or more pictures of people and places.

The floor was hardwood, but barely a couple of inches of wood shown all around the floor rug, that managed to have all chair, table, couch and bookcase legs atop the cream color based and flower patterned rug, that added to the warmth of the room. Two end tables with two small lamps flanked the couch on which we found ourselves, with a couple of "books being currently read", lying on the end tables, with bookmarks awaiting the readers' re-start.

Behind all the pictures and below of cream colored moldings, the parts of the walls that could be seen, had been painted in a rather drab light greenish color, but it really wasn't noticeable, as collectively, the parts of all four green walls that you could see, wouldn't have made up about only a couple of square feet in total. The Mayfield's used pictures as their wallpaper. The ceiling was painted a soft white, with a raised molded oval design about 3 feet wide by 5 feet in length, being the focal point of anyone looking up from couch or chair. All in all, it was a perfectly charming home, and the first one we had actually been in, with the exception of the various Bed & Breakfast places we had seen the past 40 days. However, this one represented the Mayfield's very well, so just after our 360 degree perusal of the room was completed, both Mr. and Mrs. M entered the West corner doorway at the same time, almost colliding with Henry's arms full of a tray and 4 glasses, and some English looking pastries on two plates, all of which he sat down on the small 2' x 4' wood cocktail table in front of the couch.

"Mrs. Mayfield, these are the Christian's", he stated as he stood upright after playing Butler to us. "Remember the phone call from Charles and Penelope and Broome Park?"

"Why yes, I do." She said as she approached us. "Welcome. We just love the Witherington's, so when Henry told me they were sending you here, we were so looking forward to meeting you. And in what part of America do you live?"

"We used to live in the Chicago, Illinois area for years, in a town called, Arlington. Lisa is from the North of Chicago, but I hail from the Detroit, Michigan area, where my parents still live," came my explanation. After selling my business, we moved to the West side of Michigan and purchased a farm, and we live in the farmhouse.

"We have never been to the States, so it is all strange geography to us, but we are glad you are here," she said, as she offered us a cup of tea from the small pot brought into the room by her husband. "Are you sure you wouldn't prefer some tea? Henry should have provided you with some options."

Accepting the offer, Lisa said, "I would love some, we just didn't want you to go to any trouble for us."

"Tis no trouble a'tall dearie, and you Mr. Christian? Can we convince you to try some of our fine English Tea?", she stated as she poured Jen's cup.

"Ok by me, thank you." I said, not wanting to turn down their hospitality.

"Good. Excellent," she said as she poured my cup as well. "And you Henry?"

"Not this time Deidra. I've had my 3 cups already today. I shall just enjoy my Scotch." He exclaimed, holding up his glass for self-examination, then for a toast. "To our visitors from America, by way of Broome Park!"

This segway comment was perfect as I'm sure we were all wondering how to begin the conversation for the reason for our visit to Brighton.

"Cheers." Was the only seemingly appropriate thing to say. "Cheers to us all".

"Broome Park," began Henry, as he smiled at both of us, "quite an interest place, is it not?" As we both nodded, he continued. "Please tell us how it is you came to Broome Park in the first place?"

Using his invitation to speak, all I could think of saying was, "My Uncle Patrick insisted that, if I ever came to England, make sure you visit Broome Park."

"Then your Uncle Patrick Christian had been there before?" asked Henry.

"No, not to my knowledge. And, it is my Mother's brother Patrick. Patrick Tanner. And strangely enough, his father, Leslie Charles Patrick Tanner, was born, right here in Brighton!"

"You don't say!" exclaimed Mrs. Mayfield. "Right here in our Brighton?"

"Yes, and I don't mean to add to the mystique, but his Mother's name, was Deidra. Deidra Taylor Tanner." I offered, and now waited for her response.

"Why Deidra Taylor is my name." She said softly.

Lisa chimed in, "Penelope Witherington mentioned that to us."

"Well blye me," blurted Henry. "Deidra my dear, your long-lost relatives have come back to Brighton."

Not wanting to heighten the moment, I said, "We are not suggesting that we are somehow related, but we found it quite interesting, when Penelope remembered your maiden name, Mrs. Mayfield, and …"

"Please do call me Deidra, especially now. Even if it turns out we are not related, I somehow want you two to call me Deidra. We are so glad you are here." she said, as her demeanor had now definitely turned melancholy. "To think of all this is," she started to say, but then, she began to tear up.

"Now now, Mrs. M., let's not get carried away", said Henry. "Like Mr. Christian said, it could just be coincidental."

"Yes," I offered, "and Deidra and Henry, please do call us Lisa and Evan."

"Oh my," Deidra now began to cry, "Oh my, my favorite Uncle was called Evan, and it was he who always told me, "Deidra, make sure you know about your Family Roots. They are so important to remember. It's, it's like you Evan, were destined to meet us. You see, before my Uncle Evan passed away 10 years ago, we had worked on our family lineage together. We had gone back several generations, and one of the branches of the family tree, was somehow linked to Broome Park. We never quite identified how that was possible, but we came across old family letters that referred to "The relatives' connection to Broome Park. We could never document any of this, so we just left it as branch, with no further leaves on it, so to speak. Does this make any sense to you?"

"More than you can imagine," I responded. I then took the next 10 minutes and described the Phoebe Tanner Family connection, albeit no blood connection to Broome Park ownership, but you would have thought I was touching Mrs. Mayfield's soul with each item I brought up. So, after explaining all of what I could remember, we all just sat there in a quiet peace, for what seemed like an eternity, until Henry said;

"I need another Scotch." Said Henry.

CHAPTER 8

THE TAYLOR'S AND THE TANNER'S

"So, your visit to Broome Park, was at your Uncle's suggestion. Why do you think he was so adamant about it?" asked Deidra.

I responded, "My Uncle Patrick, much like your Uncle Evan, was interested in our family's heritage. When I was in my early 20's, he created a family tree that linked the Tanner & Taylor Families of Brighton. However, it was discovering old family letters, written in the 1800's, that stated Great Aunt Phoebe became Lady Oxenden via her 1848 marriage to Sir Henry Chudleigh Oxenden, the 8th Baronet of Oxenden Baronetcy, which, since 1643, included the Estate at Broome Park."

I continued, "At first, we knew there were no

"blood ties" with the Tanners and the Oxenden's, but it was still fun thinking that one related to us, actually lived at Broome Park. However, upon further investigation, we discovered that in 1854, Aunt Phoebe bore Sir Henry's 5th child, George Chicester Oxenden. Sir Henry's first four children, were from his marriage to his first wife, Charlotte, who died soon after the birth of their 4th child."

Waiting patiently through my explanation, Henry finally interjected, "And you have proof of these occurences."

I continued, "Yes, Uncle Pat got copies of County Kent records that document everything."

"Then you are blood connected to the Oxenden's through Phoebe's son George." Stated Deidra.

"Well, if you put it that way, then yes," said Lisa.

Then I continued, "But the biggest disappointment is that Uncle Patrick could not find out what happened to Aunt Phoebe's only son, George. All we really know is that the Oxenden Family and the Baronetcy lost Broome Park just prior to or just after, World War I."

Henry then stood up, walked over to the

fireplace, and lit his pipe, while stating, "It was very common in the years surrounding The Great War, when many English Estates collapsed. The reasons were the same; Estates were expensive to maintain, Times were changing, and the War changed everything. Only the Monarchy had the financing and the Citizenry's support to perpetuate their extravagant Castles and Lifestyles."

"It is interesting that you say that Henry," I replied, "as by the time the 10th Baronet ran the family, there wasn't enough money to maintain the estate, so it was sold to Lord Kitchner, your Military Hero from World War I."

"I remember reading about that during one of our stays at Broome Park," chimed Deidra.

"Yes, but we cannot determine when Lord Kitchner gave up the Estate, and as you may know, it was used as Headquarters, during World War II, for the Royal Canadian Air Force," I added.

Henry replied, "Yes, I do remember hearing that."

After a few moments of silence, Henry then sat down once again, and looking me in the eye, he began to smile greatly, when he inquired, "Then what is it, Mr. Christian, that you experienced at Broome Park, that caused the Witherington's to send you to us?"

Smiling back and almost breathless with his question to me, I replied, "Charles told us, that You also had an interesting occurrence while visiting Broome Park?"

"Which shall we talk about first; Your experience or mine?" retorted Henry.

"How did you know I had an experience?" I said.

"I suspected as such when Charles called. Why else are you here wondering about my experience?" Henry explained.

"Let's begin with You." I said.

"I'm guessing yours' started during a heavy fog, as did mine, as did Charles Witherington's? he inquired. I nodded.

"Well it seems that FOG plays a key role in Broome Park revealing its' past to visitors. For me, it began while strolling the grounds early one June morning, when Deidra was still sleeping, and I couldn't sleep. I walked out the front door, and headed South towards the entrance to the estate, when minutes before, what I thought would be a beautiful sunrise, suddenly became a cold, damp dark walk through a ferocious fog which rolled over me like a wave on the shore."

With both Lisa and I nodding together, Henry continued, "At first, I tried to continue walking, in hopes of improving my view within the fog. However, bumping into a narrow tree, which left a knot on my forehead, changed my approach in dealing with my predicament. I decided to stay put, at least for a while, as I could not see beyond the end of my extended arms. You have heard of the English saying, "As thick as pea soup?" Well, I was swimming in the soup below the surface. In all my years of living in Brighton, which believe me, we have our share of thick fog, nothing was ever like that day in June."

I smiled and again nodded my belief in his story.

"Then, the voices started. Although they were definitely English, their tone and word sequence were strange to my ears. It was as though I had been transported to Stratford von Avon, and I was listening to two Shakespearean characters." He then acted out what happened. *My Lord twill harshly deal with me, shan't he Shamus?"* was the first voice given. *"No so Edgar. Our Lord wilt understand but his countenance is surely kind, and wilt forgive thee," came the reply.*

Then turning towards us, like he was asking for our "buy-in" of his story, he continued to share the exchange of words he heard in the fog.

"Edgar, thou hast worked here for only a fortnight and have not encountered his Lordship as often as I, so thou dost not know thy Masters' true character. He is gentle and understanding," pausing a bit before continuing the dialogue, "Surely, he may reprimand thou for thine errors, but, like our Good King Edward, he dost not allow his stature to hold unfair dominion over his subjects."

"I pray thou art correct Shamus, else I find myself outcast, and fighting for my life amongst the peasantry of England, and surely be lost to the Black Plague, like so many other unfortunates."

Again, turning towards us, Henry stated, "These are not the exact words I overheard, but do you get the jest of their comments?"

I responded to Henry by saying, "It sounds as though they are somehow Servants of someone." Henry nodded. "But, the mention of Good King Edward; to which Edward do you think are referring?"

"Well," said Henry, as he walked over to his

living room bookcase, "I referred to this book; The History of the British Monarchy, in order to precisely answer that question." Thumbing through its' pages, Henry began mumbling to himself; "Let me see, yes here it is. Edward the 1st - lived 1239 to 1307 - was Crowned 1272 and married in Canterbury in 1299, to Eleanor of Spain.......no I don't believe it was him....... and neither too, his son, Edward the 2nd, whose Wife ordered his death, placing her son, Edward the 3rd, as King, in 1327, where he reigned for 50 years, gaining love and respect from his subjects."

Pausing for a second, Henry continued, "Shamus' reference to Edward, well might indicate England's third Edward, but I can't be sure."

Listening to his dissertation, I replied, "I couldn't help but shudder when I heard the reference, to the Black Plague and..."

Quickly responding, Henry interjected, "Why yes, the Plague as well would indicate Edward the 3rd, as that took place in the mid 1300's killing one-third of England's people." Henry paused again to ponder the death of so many. "But, the timing of that Edward and Broome Park doesn't make sense, as the Estate was not built until the 1600's?"

"But Henry," I replied, "I now recall my Uncle saying something about the Baronetcy having been granted to the Oxenden Family, in the 1300's, or was it in the 1500's. I can't remember exactly. Perhaps, they lived somewhere else in County Kent or Canterbury, prior to Broome Park's construction?"

"Evan, my lad," Henry smiled, "You may be correct. In any case, we have to go back at least a couple of hundred years before we encounter English citizenry who spoke the English that I heard in the fog that day!" "But let me continue; Edward the 4th, served as King from 1461 to 1483, with that "one year of interruption" by Henry the 6th's wife Margaret and her boyfriend and Henry 6th's cousin, Warwick, although Edward has them both killed upon his return to the throne in 1471". "It sounds like there was too much going on, for him to be a great King, and of course his Sons, Edward the 5th, and Richard, were mysteriously disposed of during the 5th's first two months as King. My oh my. Such ruthless behavior, just to become a King. I do wonder what ever happened to those two 13-year old boys." Turning his eyes toward Lisa and I he exclaimed, "No one ever found the remains of them!"

"Let's continue, shall we?", as Henry dove back into his reference book. "Ok, yes, not him. Henry the 9th, that unfortunate son of Henry the 8th and Jane Seymour, was only nine years old, and under two Protectorates, during his 6-year reign, which ended with his death, due to tuberculosis, so he had no children." Henry now began to turn the books' pages more quickly, passing through historical time, like a Hollywood movie quickly scanning the centuries, before coming to a point in time worth mentioning, "Ah yes, that brings us to Edward the 7th, Queen Victoria's eldest, and the dawn of the 20th Century; far too close to our time, to have our Edgar and Shamus, speaking in a pre-Shakespearean dialect. So, Evan my boy, I believe you are correct in assuming that Shamus's "Good King" comments towards England's Edward III's link the Oxenden's, to the second to last of the 331-year reign of the House of the Plantagenets."

"I'm not sure of what you just said Henry, but you sure seem to know of your country's history." I replied.

"One thing in which we British have been well

tutored, is to know the difference between the Houses of the Windsors, the Hanoverians, the Stewarts, the Kings & Queens of Scotland, the Tutors, the Yorks, the Lancasters, the Plantagenets, the Normans, the Saxons, the Vikings, and all the way back to early Saxon Kings, right after the Romans left this land in the year 600AD." Henry stated with proud memory.

"Thank you so very much for the wonderful history lesson Henry," chimed in Deidra, "but poor Lisa and Evan, just want to know more about your mystical encounter with Broome Park, rather than England's sorted history."

"Of course, they do dear, but to understand where he and I entered the past history of Broome Park will be invaluable should either of us get STUCK IN THE PAST!" Chimed Henry.

Having been a quiet listener to Henry's dialogue, Lisa finally commented, "Any way you look at it, there seems a link to Broome Park by both Henry and Evan, as well, as Charles Witherington. However, I'm curious if you Henry, ever tried to go back to Broome Park, and hopefully again encounter another thick fog, and another step, back in time?"

"Lisa my dear, I did just that, multiple times,

but during all of those attempts, the fog experience must not have been thick enough, to somehow transport me to another time in history?", Henry replied.

Turning to me, Lisa stated, "You know Evan, we never did ask Charles Witherington, if he did try to go back again?"

Henry interjected, "If I may Lisa, Charles and I did have the same conversation, and yes, he too, tried several times to do just what you said, but to no avail for likely the same reasons as I."

I commented, "I am wondering why, he didn't stay with me, when the fog came in two days ago. It had to cross his mind, don't you think?"

Nodding in agreement, Henry replied, "Perhaps Evan, it was because going through the experience with someone he didn't know, would be awkward, or perhaps, he knew Penelope would not be for the idea, or maybe even "it" doesn't work with multiple persons present, as only a sole, lost person in the fog, is granted the opportunity to see Broome Park in another time?"

"You make sense Henry, yet I can't help but wonder how many different people, as you say, "have been entitled", to the Broome Park Experience?", came my reply, but my curiosity is certainly heightened by, not just my experience, but also with what You and Charles got to hear. I want to try to do it again."

Not needing to turn around to look at Lisa, I could tell from looking at Deidra Mayfield, who was looking at Lisa, that my wife's reaction to my desire to go back, was not being well received. Thank goodness Deidra served as a buffer to Lisa's reaction, as she stated, trying to inject humor into the moment, "Evan, I don't think Lisa thinks your thoughts are worth thinking,"

As we all turned towards Lisa, her eyes were riveted on me, though her expression didn't show anger, it certainly didn't show compliance either.

Lisa then turned from me, towards the Mayfield's as she stated, "My wonderful husband, has lost track of time, and is forgetting, that tomorrow morning, we leave from Heathrow, and return to the good old U S of A. Our forty days in Great Britain are just about over, though I too, did want to come here to Brighton and meet you nice folks and listen to what happened to you Henry. I think, like you Mr. Mayfield, that my husband, was lucky to have had "his experience" but now it is time for the Christian's of Michigan, to think about returning home to our 3 lovely children, and our regular lives….. don't you think so too, Evan?"

Henry let the moment of silence exist before he interjected, "Well, at least before you leave Brighton, please tell me Evan, exactly, what was your interlude? What time in Broome Park History did you hear, as I am assuming you didn't see much either during your experience?"

Thank goodness for Henry, as it allowed the arrows from Lisa's eyes to cease piercing the back of my neck, at least for the moment. I replied to the Mayfield's, not leaving out anything from my encounter, and Henry's response was nothing but smiles.

"What a thrill to have heard the plane crashing. I remember seeing pictures in the Broome Park Library about the Estates' role in World War II.", Henry commented with the excitement of a young history student.

I kept on with my story as Deidra and Henry hung on every one of my words. After the explanation was over, I decided to change the subject at hand, at least for the moment, and asked Henry to give me a brief history on Brighton and County Sussex and their roles in English lore. Henry granted my request and for the next 20 minutes we learned more about South, Central England than we would if we had read 20 books about the subject.

After the tea and crumpets were all consumed, the Mayfield's invited us to stay for dinner, but using Lisa's reminder of our airline travel obligations, we denied their request but gratefully thanked them for their time and hospitality. We exchanged email and resident addresses, phones and even birthdates, at Deidra's request, so I'm guessing we will get a card from the Mayfield's on my next birthday, or Lisa's, or our Anniversary, which will be quite fine with us, as they were very accommodating, to accept an "out of the ordinary visit, by two unknown American's, who might even be relatives. We discussed that aspect of being relations, and assured them that we would stay in touch, and even "scan and email" them copies of Tanner-Taylor letters from the early 1900's that proved our connections to Brighton and Broome Park. In truth, they already seemed like second or third or fourth cousins, so staying in touch was something we both wanted to do.

Henry, knowing our time schedule was limited, still wanted to make sure we at least got to see, Brighton's most famous architectural building,

"The Grand Pavillion", on the South shore of England, so after leaving 122 West Abernathy, we drove to the first street, made a left turn, and in 4 short blocks, we found ourselves in front of the Atlantic Ocean on a typical cloudy, English Sunday afternoon, with Brighton's version of "A Boardwalk" stretching from East to West, with the centerpiece of this wonderful live picture being a large and long, two stories tall, incredible Pavillion, with architectural styling having been influenced upon its' architect, so that the building looked like it belonged in India or somewhere in China. While we didn't have time to go into the building, or even get out of the car, we progressed Westward along the shoreline road, taking in the English citizenry and the many tourists, who were experiencing England's South Shore in all of its' natural beauty and historical grandeur. After, 10 minutes of sightseeing, Lisa reminded me of our schedule to return home and her desire to get a good nights' sleep at the Hotel near Heathrow, so the flight over the Atlantic would be restful and not stressful.

However, out of nowhere, just as we were ready to leave the boundary of Brighton, Lisa shouted out, "Evan, we cannot leave here without seeing the house in which your Grandpa Tanner was born!"

I replied, "Oh my goodness, you're right. We cannot possibly come to Brighton without doing so." So, turning into a residential street, I stopped the car, got out my binder of things I had brought from home, to make our trip more useful, but I had forgotten, until now, that I had included a paper that contained the address, and picture of Grandpa Tanner's birth residence, as well as the names, birthdates, marriage dates and deceased dates and offspring of all the Tanners from Brighton. Using the GPS, we saw that we were less than a mile away from Roysden (King's Den) House, on Harrington Street. Going East for a half mile, I proceeded North on Ainslet Street, which jogged to the Northeast, before again turning due East and there we were, sitting in front of the home built by my Great Great Grandfather, Frederick Tanner who was married in St. Peters Church in Brighton, England on ?-?-187? to Deidra Taylor (born May 18, 1851), who begat 5 sons and 2 Daughters, with the middle sons' name being, Charles Harry Tanner (born January 20, 1888), who married on July 13, 1912 to Mabel Stynning (born November 4, 1888), who begat Nina on August 20, 1913 and Leslie Charles Patrick Tanner on March 17, 1916, and because of the date of birth, Grandpa Tanner picked up the additional name in commemoration of Ireland's namesake Saint, which was obviously passed on to my Uncle Patrick.

For being 150+ years old, the home looked amazingly well kept. Its' simple architecture was likely common for the early 1870's for a typical Brighton neighborhood, and as I reviewed the paper I brought, with all of its' notes, I was reminded of everyone that lived here. It looks like upstairs, there might have been 3 or 4 bedrooms, so a bit of bunkbed stacking must have been utilized by Charles Harry and his 3 brothers. Perhaps Charles spent his early years sharing one of the rooms with his two older sisters, Alice Emma (born March 9, 1881) and Edith Ellen (born September 15, 1883), or the boys room contained 4 beds for William Tanner (born 11-8-1876) and George Frederick Tanner (born November 22, 1878) and Charles' two younger brothers, Earnest Alfred Tanner (born October 10, 1890) and Walter Arthur Tanner (born August 12, 1892).

Whatever the circumstances, the home

looked like a great place to live. The Patriarch, Frederick, owned and ran a Printing Business in Brighton. However, I recall my Uncle Pat stating the business wasn't big enough to support all the upcoming brothers, so the first to depart Brighton and for that matter, England, was my Great Grandfather, Charles Harry, who left the old world while still in his teens, immigrating to the British Commonwealth of Canada, settling in Montreal, where he met and eventually married Mabel at Christ Church Cathedral.

It wasn't until I looked at the documentation thoroughly, that I realized I had the information about Deidra Taylor and should have shown this to Deidra Taylor Mayfield, earlier. The papers showed Deidra's Father and Mother were William Taylor, born in 1808 and he married Susan Barnard, who was born in 1816. William was raised in Dorman Cottage in Southminster, Essex, England and we assume Deidra was raised in Brighton, as they were married in June of either 1830 or 1832, some records we have conflict the dates. IF the latter date is correct, then the 6th child of William and Susan Taylor, daughter Deidra, died just shy of age 90 on March 23, 1942, almost 110 years after the marriage of her parents. Deidra was preceded by siblings Joseph, Susan, William Jr., Mary Ann, and Ellen. She was followed by siblings George, Charles, Alfred and Harry, none of for whom we have birth, marriage, or death date data. We do know that Deidra's sister, Ellen, married a Mr. Eley, and they had a daughter, Ellen Eley born in 1876 and who in 1901 married the eldest son of Frederick Tanner and Deidra Taylor, essentially resulting in the marriage of First Cousins. Fortunately, or unfortunately, depending on your opinion of cousins who married, the couple never had children.

After a few moments of reflection on Roysden House, we began our journey back to London and home. A few comments on how to get to the M3 Highway North, was all that was said until we reached the outskirts of London, and the bypass to Heathrow. I suspect we were both reflecting on the events of the past two days and keeping our thoughts to ourselves resulted in the ensuing silence. What Lisa was truly pondering, I cannot confirm, but I kept thinking about the encounters of Henry, Charles and myself, wondering if it was possible to return to Broome Park, and hope for another heavy fog, which might set the stage for another trip back into time. But, what time? Would another encounter return me to World War II, or could I possibly get back to around the Shakespearean times, Henry seemed to have confronted. My true desire would be to hear what Charles heard; that of the mid to late 1800's, when Great Aunt Elizabeth Phoebe Tanner lived there. At least if the encounter resulted in the ability to "gain presence" in that time, rather than just be a bystander hearing other people talk, then I would have the presence of mind, to talk to Sir Henry Chudleigh Oxenden and Elizabeth and let them know that I was from the future. Not just any future, but from a future connected to the lineage of they themselves. Would I gain credence with Sir Henry by knowing of his storied past and the Baronetcy that began with his 6-time Grandfather, the original Henry Oxendin of 1312, having been granted his Title by Edward III, King of All England. I would have to keep on my person, as I went back in time, the documentation I now possessed, which I could show and share with Sir Henry, so he wouldn't think me crazy. Crazy? I must be crazy just thinking about going back. What if I went back in time successfully and couldn't return to our current year of 2020. Would I risk not seeing Lisa and the Kids again? Most certainly. But, to come this far, and to know my experience was real, through the conformation of both Mr. Witherington's and Mr. Mayfield's surreal visits to Broome Park. I may never again return to England and County Kent. And even if I did, would it be the season of heavy fog off the Cliffs of Dover, making it way towards Canterbury, soaring directly over Broome Park and the past? Likely not, so if I were to do something, it had to be here and now. And what about Lisa? Do I ask here to stay here and wait? Wait how long?

No, the answer to my decision dilemma was to place Lisa on a plane back to Michigan, and for me to extend my stay, returning to Broome Park. What would Broome Park's David Stellars and Miss Knighley and the Pro Shop Clerk, Miss Olivia say if I were to return there by myself? I could convince Olivia that I was returning to finally play the golf course in completion. I'm guessing Stellars and Knightley would ask about why my wife wasn't joining me, but regardless of the Broome Park staff, or the Mayfields, or the Witheringtons, or even Lisa and her obviously sound objections, I somehow still had to return to Broome Park and give it one more try. So, after a long period of silence, shortly after turning on to the London bypass to Heathrow, a decided to bring up my crazy plan to Lisa. But, how? How do you tell your wife, you want to go back in time, again?

The remarks came as simultaneously as possible, with both Lisa and I talking at the same time.

Lisa blurted out, "I sure hope you are not even considering, what I think you are considering, Evan Christian."

While I countered with, "Lisa, how can I come this close and consider not going back to Broome Park?"

"What?", she said, as though my comments were heard, AFTER she had made her comments. While I said the same thing, "What?"

"You cannot be serious Evan!", with her voice elevated to a level I had never heard from her before.

"Lisa, you heard both Charles and Henry, they…" as I tried to continue.

Notching up her tempo and her decibels, Lisa counters, "Are you crazy? What happens if you are successful and you do go back in time, only this time, you just don't hear voices, you, you, "you come to life" in the 1850's, or the 1350's, of the 1940's, and you cannot figure out how to come back to 2022? What do I say to our Children? What do I say to your Parents? No reports from the English Government on the disappearance of one Mr. Evan Christian of Michigan, USA. What does that make me? A wife who found a way to dispose of her husband while vacationing in Great Britain, so she could collect your $1million in Life Insurance? Now, your children would be minus a Father and have a Mother in Prison. Really Evan, you simply cannot be serious?"

I offered, "Stating it that way, you're right, you are absolutely correct. It makes no sense at all to even consider….., dropping you off at Heathrow, and returning to County Kent, to …."

"To what Evan? To meet your relatives? To possibly meet Queen Victoria, or Shakespeare or Chaucer, or Henry VIII? To change the course of history and warn England about Hitler, so they can plan accordingly? Come on Evan Christian, get real." As she rested her case.

As I continued driving, I waited a few moments for my response and then I offered her a question, "Lisa, when I first laid claim to my experience, I know you didn't believe me. But then, after dinner and then breakfast with Charles and Penelope, you began to believe, didn't you?" She didn't respond, but I continued, "And after visiting Deidra and Henry in Brighton, and his experience, I know you have to believe some of this is true; don't you?"

"Evan, it is not a matter of believing or not believing. What only matters is the potential, no the likelihood of you going back and never returning. I couldn't bear to never see you again. You just cannot be serious.", as she began to tear up from her statements to me.

"Honey, what if there is more to experience. Like you say, Canterbury Tales have been ongoing for hundreds of years. Maybe County Kent, England is a place FOR people to go back in time, what if..."

Then, I was interrupted by Lisa, "Look, I'm not prepared, nor will I ever be prepared to have you away from me, and not know exactly where you are, let alone WHEN you are! I want you to stop immediately with these crazy thoughts. We are spending the night at Heathrow and we are leaving for home tomorrow morning. Do you get that? End of conversation!"

Over our 25 years of marriage, we have had very few arguments and none that caused her to respond the way she did today, so for the moment, I decided to just continue driving to Heathrow. My mind kept working on going back, but my mouth remained closed.

CHAPTER 9

INTERNET SEARCH ON CANTERBURY TALES & COUNTY KENT

Forty Days and Forty Nights have been a part of history since time began. Noah, his Family and the surviving animals, rocked back and forth for 40 days and 40 nights, and then some, as they also waited for the water to recede before all could exit the Ark stuck on Mount Ararat in the Arabian Peninsula.

Moses walked the wilderness for 40 days and 40 nights, until he came upon the camp of his future Father-in-Law and Wife, and then some, as he waited until seeing his destiny was to climb the mountain and encounter a "burning bush".

My personal 40 days and 40 nights began 40 days ago and the 40th night was to be spent at this Hotel near London's Heathrow airport, while we awaited our 9:30 am departure on Delta Airlines to Detroit, Michigan and then a 3 ½ hour drive to 30 miles north of Muskegon, Michigan and our Family. What I began to think about, was my "personal experience, and then some", as I still wanted to return to Broome Park.

Not too many words were said on our remaining miles around London, until arriving at the car rental, where we turned in our transportation of 40 days, and caught a shuttle to the hotel. Upon checking in, Lisa just wanted to order room service, flip on the TV and eventually fall asleep.

I, on the other hand, was happy to eat via room service. Rather than watch television, I decided to open my laptop and cruise the internet.

Typing CANTERBURY TALES AND HISTORY OF THE UNEXPLAINED on to the Internet line, then pressing enter, resulted in a variety of choices, headed by "Take an Historical Phenomenon tour on High Street in Canterbury, England". The website is aimed at tourists but it also led to other searches of paranormal activity in and around County Kent, England.

What I was looking for was statistics. Statistics that would reveal if any persons have been lost without explanation, after entering the County. While most every city of any size, anywhere has had their share of "missing persons", and County Kent is no different, but nowhere on any of the websites referencing Kent Count Missing Persons, did it list Tourists who have been lost while in County Kent.

What did this mean to me? Risk aversion. I knew I had to return to County Kent, but how to break it to Lisa was the issue. So, I started with the weather forecast for Southeastern England, which showed more heavy fog expected for the next few days. That made the decision easier, as I would either be successful or be on a plane to America shortly thereafter. I went online to change just my plane reservation, without informing Lisa, while at the same time, I upgraded her to First Class, so being without me on the ride home might be a bit easier. I then rented a car and booked a room at Broome Park for the next 5 days.

While I was doing all this, Lisa was showering, so she wouldn't have to do so in the morning. By the time she was already for bed, I had changed the luggage to be all hers and all mine in the two suitcases and carry-on bags, all except what we would wear the next day. I had decided not to tell her this evening, thinking the best way to break it to her, was on the shuttle ride to Heathrow from the Hotel.

As she thanked me for such a wonderful trip, she had seemingly forgotten about my desire to return to Broome Park and nothing was said as we went to sleep. Within minutes, she was sound asleep from the hectic 40 days here, but I laid awake for some time, thinking about if and when and where I would end up in time and place, IF my actions actually got me back in time. Finally, I too was asleep, rising with the planned wake up call.

CHAPTER 10

ARGUMENTS ONLY LAST WHEN WE'RE TOGETHER

As we busily prepared to finish packing and left our hotel room for check out and shuttle ride, not much was said. However, Lisa herself broke the ice as we entered the grounds of Heathrow, when she grabbed my arm and stated, "Evan, I truly wish you could go back to Broome Park and answer this mystery yourself. I appreciate you seeing my view and not going back…."

Because I couldn't let this opportunity pass by, I said, "You are right honey, I should go back and I am going back."

"What do you mean?" She glared at me.

"Honey, I need to go back, I have to go back and

I know I will return back to you just as I am now."
I uttered as she sat motionless. "I checked on the
weather at Dover and it's the same as two days ago
for the coming few days. IF there was ever a time to
do it again, it is now! I've booked a room for myself
at Broome Park and I have rented a car and…"

"Are you insane? What am I supposed to do
while you…", she said as I interrupted.

"You're the sanest person I know. But you
heard Charles Witherington and Henry Mayfield
and you said you believed what happened to me,
actually happened, so where is the problem?" I
said with firmness.

"Yes, I heard all you did, but what if you
become missing and don't return and you….you
become a Canterville Ghost and I never see you
again?" This time with tears in her eyes.

"One thing I also checked on the internet
was the "the list of tourists" who became missing
persons while visiting County Kent. None, did
you hear that, none were listed in Canterbury
records for several decades." I said emphatically.

Our discussion continued as got to the check
in counter and I placed 4 bags to be checked,
keeping only my small carry on, which contained

the clothes I would wear at Broome Park and a few other items.

As I checked Lisa into the kiosk, I handed her ticket to her, plus the luggage receipts given me by the Delta Desk Agent, after which I led Lisa away from the counter to a bench near the security check lines. Nothing was said for what seemed like minutes, until I grabbed her hand, looked her in the eye and stated, "I know for certain, that Uncle Pat wants me to do this", as she rolled her eyes and turned her head, I continued, "and I know I am going to come back, with only a day or two at most of time passing in current time, no matter how long I remain in the past."

"And what makes you so certain of this?" she said.

"I just know it and all I am asking is for you to trust me." I pleaded.

With more exasperation she responded, "And when I get back to Michigan, what do I tell our children and your parents?"

"I've already emailed Mom and Dad, telling them you are returning alone, and I will be back within the week, as an incredible business opportunity arose upon meeting a banker named

Charles Witherington, whom I met while playing golf at Broome Park." As I explained. "You can taxi from the airport in Grand Rapids to Muskegon and be with them by 4 PM today."

"Evan Christian, you are insane!" as she continued, "I'm not going without you, so we can just go back to the ticket counter and cancel my flight and I will go with you to Broome Park!"

"What about the kids? And my Parents?" I asked.

"We can tell call them in 5 hours and ask if they mind if we stayed two extra days", she smiled as she came and hugged me. "That's what I will give you, ONE TRY, and by God, you had better come back as you did before."

My silence didn't last for long, as I was not about to let this gift horse pass me by. It took us a good 60 minutes to retrieve our baggage as we had to give the airlines a solid reason for our cancellation. Besides, Lisa confided that it was her plan to ensure we would be back here at Heathrow, within two days, as her thoughts were that the fog would eventually have to lift and I would be back in 2022 England, instead of 1820 or whenever.

After rebooking our tickets for two days from now, we shuttled to the car rental and began our trip to Canterbury and it was noon, when we entered County Kent.

CHAPTER 11

WELCOME BACK MR. & MRS. CHRISTIAN

As we passed Canterbury and then South on the A2 Highway, I could see in the distance that fog was covering Broome Park, just as had been forecasted. However, as we approached the Broome Park exit, it was 12:30 and the fog was lifting. Another five minutes and then we passed through the Estate entrance and began the long drive up to the front door.

As though we were members of the Oxenden Family returning by horse and carriage from London, both Miss Knightly and Mr. Stellars stepped out the front door as our car came to a stop.

Stellars spoke first, "Hello again Mr. & Mrs. Christian. Miss Knightly and I just happened to be looking outside as you were coming up the drive, and since you are the only guests who have yet to check into today, we assumed it was you. Welcome back."

"Thank you", came from both Lisa and I, as we opened the trunk, lifting the luggage to the ground but before that happened...

Up stepped a 20 something Bell Boy, "Hello Mr. Christian, I'm Alec. Please let me handle that for ye sir," he said in a Scottish accent. I relented and shut the trunk and parked the car as the other three entered the front door to check us in. As I walked back towards the front door, both the other Scotsman, Mr. Dunston and the Pro Shop's Miss Olivia were standing by the side entrance and they smiled and waved at me, saying, "Welcome back Mr. Christian." The place is truly incredible. They must hire only people with super memories.

Once inside, Lisa was just finishing signing us in, while Alec was poised at the staircase with both our bags and up the stairs we went. Lisa looked at me and said, "If you can believe it, they assigned us the same room as before."

"Nothing surprises me about Broome Park," I replied.

Inside the room, we began unpacking and then looked out the South Window, watching the fog totally recede from the South half of County Kent. "The weather is supposed to do the same thing the next two days, so let's do some further investigating of the house and grounds," I suggested.

"Well first, I'm getting some lunch. You've forgotten, we haven't had anything to eat since the coffee and Danish at the hotel this morning. I'm starving," Lisa insisted. And back out our room door we went, but this time, I led us the other way down the hallway, so we could see where it went. Broome Park's 2nd and 3rd floors, seemed very similar, as both had hallways that wrapped around the inside of the building. There were eight to ten rooms on each floor, which had windows looking out towards the grounds, while about 4 rooms did not have any windows, unless they looked at an internal courtyard, but having not noticed any such courtyard on our first visit, I had to figure out what these rooms looked like. After two hallway left turns, we noticed the Chambermaid's stand outside an open door to an internal room. Knocking, I fully opened the door and called out, "Hello, anyone in here?"

"Yes sir," came the reply from a middle-aged woman, who walked out the bathroom door, with a smile on her face. "Can I help ye sir?", indicating she too was of Scottish descent.

"Hello Mam, we were just curious as to what the internal rooms looked like at Broome Park. We are in 302 and are just exploring," I sheepishly replied, so as to not appear like a thief.

"Not a problem sir, the couple checked out this morning and I'm just cleaning the room for the next guests. Feel free to explore, although the only view is of the air shaft separating all the internal rooms," came the Maid's invite.

As I looked out the window, I noticed it was offset from the other internal rooms, so guests would get some light in their room, but not be embarrassed by accidentally being discovered by other guests looking out their windows. Below was the top of the first floor, which had ported skylight glass, which gave light to the internal rooms on the first floor. Perhaps these were the first floor's staging areas, when Broome Park was an estate prior to World War I, as undoubtedly the original kitchen and staff quarters were in the basement. In the 1990's, the building was renovated. It was likely the rooms below were modified for employees to service todays' guests, but the skylights still provided light for those rooms. That allowed for the basement to have a swimming pool and exercise room installed to attract 20th and 21st Century customers.

"I'm all finished here sir," said the Maid.

"Oh, yes. Thank you very much, it is interesting in how the light gets to the 1st floor internal rooms," I commented. I asked, "What are the rooms directly below us?"

"Well, in the front half of the building, the first floor has the Lounge, Restaurant, Ballroom and Offices, while the back half contains the Kitchen, Supply Rooms, Laundry and Employee Break Rooms. 'Tis a dandy of a building, isn't it sir? She replied.

"It truly is," I said. I only wish I could have seen the Estate before the renovations, to see how the Family lived back when."

"Ah, yes sir. It must have been grand." She said as we all exited the room. "Make sure ye take the back stairs and then come back to the front of the house through the Ballroom. It 'tis so beautiful."

Looking at her name tag, Lisa said, "Thank you Fiona, you've been so kind to us."

"Happy to do so Mrs.," she said as she curtseyed and pushed her cart to the next room. "Have a wonderful stay."

We proceeded towards to back staircase looking forward to viewing the ballroom and other things we hadn't noticed during our first visit. Reaching the back stairs, even though they were half the width of the front entrance stairs, they were still grand as far as we were concerned. The wood rails and supports proved that in the 1634 the architect/builder tried to make every inch of the edifice stand on its' own as unique and luxurious. The guests of the Oxenden Family, spending a weekend at Broome Park, must have been delighted with every detail in every room of this fabulous building. Walking down the staircase, we came upon an intersection of hallways. Towards the North, were two hallways separated by a six foot wide space which must have housed the heating and electrical systems, while two more halls went East and West, to service those parts of the house, and going in the opposite direction of the down staircase, were two additional hallways, which we followed for 15 feet until we came to two traverse hallways, also going East and West, so we went right as we saw the sign for the Ballroom.

As we opened the door, the room was bright with light from the West, which came through the rooms' 4 large windows, allowing to illuminate this 40' long by 20' wide, wood floored, 20' high room. The magnificent ceiling was adorned with sculpted panels and paintings, making it the most fascinating room at Broome Park. As we strolled across the room towards the windows, two staff members entered from the North doors, smiled at us and began setting up the room, evidently for some occasion later today. We smiled back and continued our exploration, noticing several pictures on the walls of this magnificent room.

One picture showed the Building, just East and South of our Room, which was the one with the pond behind it, where I had my second "time back" experience. It was interesting to note that the pond featured children playing in the water, just as I had heard before. Another picture captured the West View out of the house, with the gently sloping terrain, coming to the property line, where Charles had heard one of the Oxenden's returning to Broome Park's boundaries.

Still another was a painting of the North View from the back of the Estate, showing the "grazing area" for Broome Park's many animals that donned the farm portion of the land.

While the "turn of the 20th century magazine articles", Uncle Patrick had given me, showed Portrait Paintings of the various Sir Henry's and Wives, had originally hung in the front parlor and family dining rooms of Broome Park, I was disappointed to not see any hanging anywhere in the building at this time. Perhaps, it was to protect them from would be thieves, but if they were hanging in their original places, it would truly make one feel, that "Broome Park, the Family Home", was still in tack after nearly 400 years of existence.

In any case, we were Broome Park and I was ready for the next adventure. Where and When I was going, I did not know, but as we reached our room after our tour of the house, I decided to dress as drably as I could, in case I went back in time, and actually got to make contact with someone. Why I had bothered to bring, this one, long sleeved, dark blue tee shirt was beyond me, but it fit the bill perfectly, as I needed something, that would not make me "stand out" like a sore thumb, as would a Polo or Under Armor Shirt would do. For slacks, I chose my dark beige khaki's, that had no cuffs, as these were the only clothes that would make me look like an ordinary citizen of County Kent, at least for the last 150 years. If I went back further in time, I'd be out of luck, as I had no "tights", to make me blend in with the attire of the 18th century or before. Who was I kidding? If, I do make contact, and they examine my clothes, how can I explain the Dockers, name tag on the inside of my pants, and the 36" x 34" size tag, so I cut them out, along with the tag for the tee shirt, which fortunately, didn't have any printing on it like Detroit Tigers, or Chicago Cubs.

Even though it was now just past 3 pm, due to County Kent's latitude, there would still be plenty of daylight left to give the Pro Shop the impression that I was here to finish my round of golf from a few days ago. I just had to make one more check of the afternoon's weather, to see if the fog would still come upon Broome Park. While in our room, and waiting for my laptop to complete opening, I couldn't help but look up and see tears coming from Lisa's eyes, as she worried about my upcoming effort to go back in time.

"Honey", I said, "Everything is going to be alright. I'm excited. The weather report looks like the heavy fog will be hear in another hour or so, so now is the time!"

Lisa said nothing as I walked over to hug her before leaving the room to go to the Pro Shop. I took a small duffle bag to store in my golf bag, which had my brown walking boots and a jacket in case it was needed. I wore my spikeless golf shoes and the jacket to cover up the drab attire underneath, so as to not expose my lack of golfing fashion to Broome Park's Golfing Employees.

As I opened the door, Lisa softly said, "I love you Evan Christian. Don't forget to come back." I smiled and responded, "I love you too. I'll see you in less than 2 days." And, off I went to the greatest adventure of my life.

CHAPTER 12

GOLFING, THE 2ND TRY AT BROOME PARK– WHAT WILL HAPPEN?

As I entered the Pro Shop, I was greeted again by the smiling Olivia, who said to me, "Mr. Christian, we're ready for your Tee Time, but I feel we must say to you, that the heavy fog, is again expected this afternoon, so going out to play has to be your decision. The golf course has just a few groups on it as we speak, and they have only a few holes left to play, as most others, decided not to go out this afternoon, due to the expected conditions."

"Thank you for letting me know this Olivia, and I understand. At least this time, I know what to expect. I have my mobile phone and a jacket in case it gets colder like last time, but I'm excited to go play the rest of the holes. After all, I was Level Par for the first five holes, last time, so if Mr. Dunston, can drive me out to the 6th Tee, perhaps, I will start there and finish more quickly", I explained.

"If that's what you like, Mr. Dunston, is just outside, as he is ready to leave for the day, as his work is done, and I'm sure he would be happy to accommodate you.", came Olivia's reply.

As Olivia and I exited to Shop, the smiling Mr. Dunston, was there in his greenskeeper cart, as he had heard I wanted again to play, despite the possible fog. "Mr. Christian. I canna advise you enough, that you will likely encounter the same fog, as ye had last time, but if it's what ye wanna do, then, I wish ye guud luck," he said.

Olivia countered, "Mr. Dunston, if you could drive Mr. Christian out to #6 tee, he said, he would start there as that is how far he got last time. Then, maybe he could finish in time."

"If that's what ye want, Mr. Christian, then hop in my cart with 'yer bag and trolley and off we'll go!" he said.

I waved to Olivia and also to Miss Knightly, who happened by, as we drove away. Mr. Dunston continued "his advisement" during our 10-minute drive out to #6 Hole. As we approached the Tee, Dunston said, "I wish I could ride along with you, so as to get ye back quickly once the fog comes in, but my wife is expecting me and…"

I interrupted, "Mr. Dunston, I truly thank you for your concern, but I'll be fine, even if I have to stop a while because of the fog. Please go on home and be with your wife and thanks again."

"OK Mr. Christian. But, please notice, you can see the fog coming over the Building as we speak. I'll be lucky to get back to the Clubhouse before it disappears. Good luck, Sir." Said Dunston as he drove off.

Looking back towards the building, I could see he was right, and this was just what I wanted. I figured before I got to #8, it would be pea soup again. After a few practice swings, I launched a surprisingly good drive, considering no warmup at all. A wedge to 20 feet and I barely missed my birdie putt. After my tee shot on #7, I was now perpendicular to the rolling fog, as I watched it while I walked towards my tee shot, which had caught the left rough. I used a 7 iron to reach this two tiered green and actually wished the fog would hold off until I finished the front nine, as I canned my 15' putt to get me to 1 under for my "combined 7 holes of play". I knew I would have to come play here again another day, if only to experience a complete, uninterrupted 18 holes. This, however, was not that day, as before I reached the 8th fairway, the fog dropped like the tent of a circus, which was closing down for day.

It was a fascinating view. Looking North, towards Canterbury, the sky was blue, with some cloud cover. Looking West the sun was still 45 degrees from the horizon, but in a matter of seconds, the rolling fog, made that sun disappear, and seconds later, it engulfed me, just as I reached the weather shelter, just off the 8th tee box. Rather than being scared and wondering what was happening, like I did the last time, I was filled with anticipation, with what might happen. I never bothered to think that maybe nothing will happen and I that I might have to sit here in the fog for a couple of hours until it dissipates.

So, there I sat on a wooden bench, under a roof, which like before, I could not even see as the fog duplicated my first experience. I quietly waited and listened. The first time, I can recall, before the fog had reached me, that I could hear the rumble of heavy trucks on the A-2, just east of the golf course. However, this time, I didn't hear anything. No trucks, no golf carts, no golfers walking and talking as they played. No bird sounds. Nothing! Would it happen again, or I have I just wasted 2 days of hotel fees, meals and air travel changes? What was I thinking? More silence.

To pass the time, I switched my golf shoes for my walking boots, and as I was tying the laces, for some reason I noticed the ring on my left ring finger. Unless I were to duplicate going back to World War II time, if it was much earlier than that, gold wedding rings, wouldn't be common for average folks, so I quickly whispered, "Sorry Lisa.", as I removed my ring and placed it in the plastic zip lock bag, which also contained some of the documents I had from Uncle Pat about Broome Park and its' inhabitants over the years. I folded the bag and its' contents and put it in my front pants pocket, just after placing my golf shoes in my golf bag, and I rolled the trolley and bag to a group of heavy bushes, and pushed everything to the center of the vegetation, so no one from another time, might come across my trolley & bag.

No, sooner had I done this, then the fog began to lift. I was amazed at how fast it lifted and literally dissipated before my eyes as I followed it skyward. The sun began to shine again, and suddenly the sky was blue again. I got up off the bench and exited the weather shelter and looked Southeast towards Broome Park and all of its' magnificence. With the sun brightly shining on the building, it somehow looked newer than it had during the cloudiness of when I drove away with Mr. Dunston.

"Oh well," I said to myself, it looks like it's not going to happen today. The fog wasn't thick enough or something. So, I disappointingly turned around to get my golf bag and trolley and return to the Pro Shop or keep playing.

Where'd it go? There was no golf bag or trolley in the bushes. There was no weather shelter. There was no hole #8. No Tee Box. No Fairway. No Green. Looking west and south there were not any other fairways or greens; only gently sloping grasslands with a few more trees than I first noticed when looking in that direction. There was no number 7 green behind me, nor fairways or greens anywhere. What the Heck?

As I looked towards Broome Park again, in the area next to where number 1 green had been, I saw and heard a group of people. A big group of people. Perhaps a few hundred. Even though I was 400 - 500 yards away from them, I could hear them, like I could hear a bunch of people in a sports stadium that far away. I walked in a "bee-line" towards the group and in doing so I encountered a small forest of trees, in a slight depression of the land, so as to make me walk down a hill to get through the trees, before walking up the hill and out of the trees and to this large group, whose conversations were getting louder with every step I took towards them.

For some reason, before exiting the forest, I instinctively removed my jacket, as the air temperature was well into the 70's. I left the jacket in a heavy bush at forest's edge.

Could it be? Could they be? As I got within 100 yards of them, their talking got louder and their clothing became more visible. So did their faces, hair and hats and…. Oh, my God.

Surrounding the group of people were horses and carts; some by themselves, some connected, but nonetheless, horses and carts. Looking further South and just to the East of Broome Park, I noticed several carriages. Fancy carriages, with what appeared to have footman attending them. I then refocused on the large group of people as I got within 50 yards of them, when one of the men saw me, and hoisted, what looked to be a pewter mug, as he said to me, "Come on lad, join the festivities!"

Before I knew it, I was part of the crowd, who all seemed to be in a celebratory mood, with almost everyone but the children, drinking from their own pewter mugs, which, from the smell, apparently contained beer!

No one seemed to really notice me, as drinking, laughing and merriment seemed to be the demeanor of the entire group. Next, someone stuck a mug in my hand, clicked it with their mug and said, "Drink up Lad! Drink to Sir Henry and Lady Elizabeth!"

Dear God, it had happened. I was here, Broome Park in the 19th Century, as best I could tell from everyone's clothes. They didn't look like garb from the 1700's, nor the late 1800's; turn of the century styles.

Out of nowhere came the question, "Where did you get the fine shirt and pants?" The same man who gave me the mug, said to the woman, "Awe Ducky, leave the boy alone, who cares what he's wearing." Then, turning to me, he said, "Have another drink."

"Don't mind William," said the woman, "I just like yer clothing. You looks nice." Then, pointing to the man, "Billy dresses like a bum, even on Sunday's. It's good to see a lad, who celebrates with the proper clothing. Here, let's make another toast to Sir Henry and Lady Elizabeth!" as she clicked her mug to mine and turned back towards the crowd.

CHAPTER 12-A

NEVERTHELESS, I WAS A STRANGER

It was still hard to comprehend. I had transitioned through the fog into the mid 1800's. Could it possibly be the time when Sir Henry Chudleigh Oxenden, the 8th Baronet of Broome Park, and Elizabeth Phoebe Tanner were living here? Is it them whom they were toasting?

Though I was no expert in English dialect, could it be they were talking in the language of Charles Dickens? I had read enough of Great Expectations, A Christmas Carol and Oliver Twist to know how Charles Dickens made mid-19th century English Commoners sound.

What were they celebrating? What year was this? I had to know. I tapped William on the shoulder, and clicked his mug and said, "Billy, so I can remember to tell to my grandchildren one day, please tell me, what day is it today?"

Laughing and pointing at me, "You'd better not let the Master know you already forgot his Second Wedding Day, God Rest Lady Charlotte. Today is August 5th, 1848. Sir Henry and Lady Elizabeth just returned from their Honeymoon, after their wedding on July 28th, at St. George's Hanover Square Westminster Church in Middlesex. To the Master!"

Re-clicking William's mug, I smiled and said, "To the Master!"

Mingling, and walking through the crowd, I couldn't believe it. Not only did I come back in time, but to the day our Family Linked to the Oxenden's! As I kept walking, all of a sudden, two arms were around my neck, and two lips were on mine. "Hello Handsome. Who are you?"

Shocked by the turn of events, I separated us and said, "Hello yourself. I'm brand new to Broome Park. Sorry I do not know you."

"We can remedy that before the day is over Ducky!", she seductively responded. "I'm Vanessa. And you?"

"I'm Evan." I said out of desperation.

"Evan? Evan? Never heard of an Evan before. Evan of where, Evan of Who?

"Evan Christian." I said.

"Evan of Christian? Where is Christian?" She replied.

"The Christian name is from Norway." Was the only thing I could think of saying.

"Are you a big and strong Viking?" She smiled and said, "Give me another kiss Ducky." As she again put her arms around me.

"Get your hands off my Vanessa." Came the angry response from a guy who was obviously drunk and had interest in Vanessa, as he took a swing at me. Fortunately, I dodged the punch and help him up as he was stumbling. "She mine!", He added.

"Who said I'm yours?" Replied Vanessa as she again tried to embrace me. "Besides Ducky he is new hire and I'm just welcoming him to Broome Park."

William helped separate Vanessa and I, as well as hold back the angry boyfriend. I thought, "Holy cow, what have I got myself into?" All eyes from the large group were now focused on the scuffle and the newcomer; Me! This was not the way I intended on easing my way back in time.

"What is going on here?" Came the inquiry from a deep voice of authority. "You shant be disturbing to Masters' Celebration like this." Looking at my attacker, he said, "Ollie, you keep your fighting to yourself." Then, turning to me, he asked, "And whom might you be Hercules?"

What do I do now? How should I respond? Dear Lord, help me get through this I prayed. "My name is Evan Christian, good sir. I would be please to meet you."

"What is an Evan Christian?" He asked.

Oh boy, this isn't starting off well, I thought. "Sir, I am not from County Kent, but I have been traveling around England for some time now.

"Why do you keep calling me Sir. I am not a Sir. Only Sir Henry can be called Sir. I am Mr. Reeves and I am Sir Henry's Head Butler. Why are you here?" Said Mr. Reeves, as the crowd had now stopped celebrating in order to listen in on the comments from Mr. Reeves.

"As I said, Mr. Reeves, I've been traveling throughout England, and visiting as many Estates as possible, to talk to the head of each estate." Was all I could come up with.

"If you've been traveling, where is your Coach, or your Horse, or your baggage?" Inquired

Reeves. "And, how did you just "happen" on to the property?"

"I was on my way from Canterbury to Brighton, and the people at the Inn in Canterbury, told me which roads to take to get here." I invented.

"So, you're trespassing?" Reeves stated. "And, who in Canterbury told you how to get here? I know most of the Innkeepers there and they wouldn't send you here unless they knew you were expected! You're nothing but a vagrant wonderer." As he grabbed my arm, "Edmond?" he said as he turned to the crowd.

A rather large male broke through the crowd to where we were standing, "Yes, Mr. Reeves?"

Looking at me, but with his head tilted towards the enforcer, Reeves said, "Edmond, please accompany our unwelcomed guest to the West Gate, so he can continue his, so called, journey to Brighton."

Immediately, my arm was besieged with the strongest grip I had ever felt, as he began to push me out of the surrounding crowd.

"Wait." I pleaded. "First, It is because of Brighton and Lady Elizabeth that I am here." Was all I could think of saying.

"How do you know Lady Elizabeth?" Came

the booming comment from Reeves, as he looked more stern than ever. "Halt Edmond" He cried, as the enforcer was still dragging me westward. Walking towards me, with the crowd following, he said, "My dear Mr. Christian, if that is truly your name, trespassing can be punishable by death, if the Master feels the intent of your being here is to do harm to anyone at Broome Park. And based on your attire, you cannot be someone who would know Lady Elizabeth, so instead of casting you off Broome Park, I think we will do something different. Edmond, take our vagrant to the stockade, as I will go to the Master and get his permission to exterminate this pest!"

Now being dragged in the opposite direction by Edmond, I cried, "How do you know I am not telling the truth?" As I shook free of Edmond and stood my ground. "If you have me killed and later Sir Henry finds out why I came here and who I am, it might not be what he wants."

Pausing to think a moment, Reeves reflected on my comments, turned towards Edmond and me, and said, "I will mention this to the Master, but in the meantime, you'll wait in the stockade." Then, he turned to the crowd to inform them, "Good people of Broome Park, I apologize for this encounter dampening your celebration, but indeed, I think it is time for us all to get back to our chores, as I will need to address this issue with Sir Henry. Please don't bother yourselves with this matter, as it will be resolved one way or another. Thank you for your joyful participation. I'm sure the Master appreciates all the good wishes. Now again, please return to your duties."

Turning to Edmond, he motioned towards the set of buildings east of us, which was all Edmond needed to continue his grip on me. The several hundred yards didn't take as long as it did for Reeves to walk his two hundred yards back to the house. As the building housing the stockade was part of a complex of buildings, most of the crowd was following us, and their chatter about me continued until we arrived at the brick building, with a heavy wooden door, strengthened by iron crossbars, meant to lock the door into the brick wall, prohibiting any jailbirds' efforts from trying to escape. After withdrawing a chain of keys from his pocket, and opening the locked door, he motioned me inward, and as he was shutting the door, he looked down at my feet, and said, "Those are interesting boots you are wearing. You surely did not get them in Canterbury. Just where are you from?"

Looking down at my boots myself, and then back up at him, I said with a smile, "Edmond, my friend, you wouldn't believe me if I told you." And with that, the door slammed shut, got locked and off he walked as I could her everyone's steps and whispers until they diminished. Turning around, I viewed my new, hopefully, temporary quarters, complete with a small "stump" stool in one corner, a batch of hay or straw spread about the ground floor for about 5 feet by 2 feet and one iron can, in the other corner, which I'm guessing was the rooms' version of a Kohler toilet. Actually, considering everything, it wasn't a bad environment, and from the scratchings on the bricks, it was used periodically, probably with an unruly employee who may have gotten drunk and needed time to himself.

So down I went on the straw, as I did my best to gather some hay as a pillow as I laid there staring at the brick and wood beamed ceiling wondering how all this transpired. Rather than feeling like a prisoner, I smiled, reconfirming my delight that, here I was back in 1848, with a chance to meet my distant relatives. What would

I tell them? How do I explain my existence to them? They could easily just think me insane and carry out Reeves explanation of what is done to unwelcomed trespassers. Suddenly, my smile, turned upside down.

Then, I thought of Lisa, either sitting in our Room, or having a meal. Think of it. Both She and Sir Henry & Lady Elizabeth may be in the same house, at this moment. It's just two alternate periods of time. They could be sitting on the same couch in the same parlor room at the same time. I smiled at the possibilities.

Meanwhile, back in Broome Park, Reeves needed to explain a situation. "Your Lordship?" Reeves asked as he entered the main parlor, which contained Sir Henry, Lady Elizabeth, and a few of the guests, who had journeyed with them, back to Broome Park, after the Wedding at St. Georges.

"Sorry to intrude your Grace", begging their pardon.

"Not at all Reeves", Sir Henry said as he rose to Reeves entrance. Turning to his guests, Henry commented, "Reeves has been Broome Park's faithful Head Butler for 22 years now, as he succeeded my Father's Butler, Robert Stone, who was Reeves Uncle, and Broome Park's faithful Butler for 54 years. What has kept this property successfully prospering for 205 years is the wonderful service our staff has provided my family and our guests." He then, turned towards Reeves.

"Thank you for the kind comments, my Lord." Said Reeves; reverently bowing. And once Sir Henry was within whispering range, he continued, "Your Lordship, during the celebration outside…"

"Ah, yes, Reeves. Are they enjoying themselves?" Henry inquired.

"Yes, my Lord, they did have a grand time, and in fact, the party just broke up as everyone is back at their duties, as we have things to prepare for you and your guests." Reeves explained. "However, your Grace, during the celebration, an intruder, who states he was on his way from Canterbury to Brighton, just "happened" on the property and…"

"Did you say Brighton, Reeves?" came the inquiry from Lady Elizabeth, who was closest to us and obviously was curious about Reeves talk with Henry. She walked over to her new husband to listen in on the conversation.

Turning to the new Head Lady of the

Household, "Yes, My Lady. But in truth, I suspect," turning back to Sir Henry, "that he is just a wondering vagrant who may have seen our celebratory group on the main lawn, as he was walking by the upper northwest hill to the property, and decided to come down, for God knows what purpose. In my opinion Sir Henry, I think he is a trespasser, who is looking for a handout, or worse."

"Then, grant him some food and send him on his way." Henry stated, as he prepared to return to conversation with his guests.

"I will your Grace. It is just that he says he knows both You and Lady Elizabeth." Reeves explained as he looked directly into the Lordship's eyes, as Henry abruptly turned back to Reeves.

"A vagrant says he knows us?" Came the reply.

"Yes, your Grace. As I was having Edmond Swaine, take him to the west gate, the intruder pleaded that he knew you and came here to see you both." Reeves awaited Sir Henry's response, but a long pause, Reeves continued, "So, I had Edmond place him in the stockade and came directly to you Sir."

"Knows me?" The puzzled Baronet mumbled. "How could someone, who appears to be a commoner, say he knows me? Reeves, how is he dressed?"

"Like a commoner Sir, although I must admit, I have never seen, a shirt such as his." Stated Reeves,

"What do you mean?" His Grace inquired.

Reeves continued, "To begin with, it has no lace ties around the top of his shirt. Rather, it looks as though it has been tailored to just be a continuous circle cut from the top of the shirt, so that the head has to "pop through" the opening, as someone would be placing on their person. And the color of the shirt is unlike any I have ever seen. It is a dark blue, with long sleeves, again with no ties or frills around the cuffs. And his pants are also of an unfamiliar color and tailoring, yet his boots seem extremely well tailored, with lacing coming up the front of both boots. Certainly, his clothing is not anything I have ever witnessed your Grace."

"Interesting. And you say you placed him in the stockade?" Henry asked.

"Yes, your Grace," Was the reply.

"Did Edmond check to see if he might be carrying a weapon of sorts?" Henry asked.

"I'm sorry to say, that I had not thought of

it your Grace, but just before I came in the side door of the house, I looked back to the stockade and saw Edmond locking the door." Stated the embarrassed Butler.

"Thank you, Reeves, for bringing this to my immediate attention. What I suggest is that Edmond and two others, go into the stockade and ensure any potential weapon is removed from our unwelcomed guest, and I shall deal with him after our guests have had their dinner and the children are put to bed. I don't want any of them to be inconvenienced by whomever this intruded may turn out to be." Said Sir Henry emphatically.

"As you say your Lordship." Said Reeves, as he bowed and left the room.

Turning to his new bride, Sir Henry stated, "Dear Elizabeth, I'm sorry that on your first day in your new home, that you have to be bothered by such business."

Elizabeth, still interested in the situation says, "But Henry, how do you think this person could possibly know both of us?"

"He could be anyone. As Reeves says, a vagrant, or perhaps he read of our marriage and he may have nefarious plans, or he just happened by and was in need of food. I truly doubt we know him, unless, my dear," smiling at his new bride, "you have a hidden lover from the past, that is jealous that you are now betrothed to me?"

Smiling back at Henry, "You shouldn't joke of such things. Has anything like this ever happened before?"

"My dear, many times we have had people come onto Broome Park, who have lost their way on their journey to Dover, Canterbury, Brighton, or elsewhere. Some were truly lost, while others were just hungry. We even have a few of our employees who did just that; wondered onto the property, we fed them, listened to their story, and hired them." Explained Henry.

"You are truly a gracious man, my love, to accommodate even those you have not known. I love you even more hearing of your kindness to others." Smiled Elizabeth.

"The Oxenden's have had good fortune for hundreds of years. We certainly didn't earn this land on our own. The first Sir Henry, back in the 1300's, was gifted his Baronetcy by Edward III, and he was astute enough to know he should appreciate all he had been given. My Father and his many Father's before him, have passed down to each generation, that good fortune is to be valued. More importantly, the responsibility to our Family, our Servants, the Community, our Country and its' Citizens, is a gift we must pass on to whomever we meet." Henry stated with humble pride. "Furthermore, it is our job, Yours now, and mine as always, to ensure that my children with Charlotte and any children that God may bless us with, will not become spoiled, due to their good fortune, but rather they learn appreciation for their circumstances and also learn how to give back to others. I wish you could have known Father. He taught me so much, and he instilled in me to do the right things. I'm lucky to now have you to help me continue this tradition of kindness."

"Oh Henry," Elizabeth said with tears in her eyes, "I am so lucky to have met and fallen in love with you. I pray God continue his blessings on Broom Park and the Oxendens. I would love to meet with this person, now in the stockade to see if he truly knows us or is looking for a handout or something else. I want to be part of the good work your family has done for years."

"OK, my dear, as you say. Now let's get back to our guests and the children. I love you deeply." Henry said as he kissed Elizabeth's cheek.

CHAPTER 12-B

MEETING THE OXENDEN'S

As hosts, Henry and Elizabeth, re-entered the parlor, all faces turned towards the newlyweds, with inquiring looks, as to what Mr. Reeves, was bringing to the Masters' attention, so soon after their arrival back home. The Oxenden wedding had been a delight. St. George's Church in Hanover Square, Winchester, has been the site of many "Upper Class" and even a few "Royal Weddings" over the years, and Elizabeth was the new talk of English Society, having been raised more of a "commoner" from Brighton, despite that fact that her Father and His Father, were "Gentlemen", meaning they had Fixed Incomes, off of which they lived. Even so, those nearest to

Royalty, tended to look down on status seekers from families, they felt, were less worthy to be included in the upper echelons of society.

To them, a pretty face and slender figure, should not provide automatic entry to relationships, that their families had enjoyed for years or even centuries. However, Elizabeth's innocent personality, kept her from the slings and arrows thrown at the wedding reception, by those jealous of her good fortune of marrying the 8th Baronet of a distinguished Baronetcy that had been granted the Oxenden's years before by Edward III.

Attendees to the nuptials, included family, friends and a variety of Royalty, as Henry Oxenden, the 7th Baronet, had been a respected and involved Member of Parliament and English Society. The Groom was especially glad to have as his best man, his longtime Oxford Classmate and Friend, the 3rd Earl of Carnarvon, Henry, whose family legacy went all the way back to 749AD. Over the centuries, the Carnarvon Estate had seen numerous wonderful edifices used as home to the Carnarvon Family. However, the year Sir Henry Chudleigh Oxenden, the 8th, and his first wife, Charlotte, gave birth to their first son, Henry the 9th, his best friend, Henry Carnarvon, was welcoming to the British landscape a birth of a building, which rivaled any before, that wasn't linked directly to Royalty. Certainly, the Windsor Castles, Kensington Palaces, and Scotland's Holyrood, were structures beyond belief and in a class by themselves. But British Nobility had always wanted their individual homes, to be something of which they could be proud.

Various British Castles, not connected directly with Royalty, dotted each of England's County's across the country. The Dixwell-Oxenden's had Broome Park built in 1643, and it stood proudly in the middle of Kent County for all to admire the past 200+ years. However, a few weeks before getting married, Broome Park's owner paid a visit on his best man, to see for himself, how the new Carnarvon home was coming.

Upon entering the 5,000 acre estate 8 kilometers south of Newbury, Berkshire, in Hampshire, just 60 miles west of London, Sir Henry marveled at the transformation of the Estate Sir Henry had seen 6 years before. Certainly, the last Carnarvon home, which had been built in 1679, represented the family wealth, but, the new home, Highcleer Castle, was a marvelous structure, which even Sir Henry was honest with his slight jealousy of the new house of his best man. There years at Oxford developed a strong bond between the two.

With Lord Henry by his side last week at St. George's Church, Sir Henry wanted his friend to be equally proud of his friend's impression of Broome Park. Therefore, among the visitors for "post wedding partying", was the 3rd Earl of Carnarvon, and his pretty wife, Priscilla. Also present were Oxford classmates, Trevor Hainsworth, the cousin of the Duke of Wellington, and wife Trudy, as well as Elizabeth's Sister, and Maid of Honor, Mary Tanner, and her current boyfriend, Robert Trentworthy, a respected Sussex county Barister. The Law is something the Sir Henry had studied at Oxford, but never put into practice, as his duties as Baronet and the running of Broome Park, prevented him from completing his legal studies. However, Sir Henry's younger Brother, Robert, who attended Cambridge 5 years after Henry's pursuits at Oxford, allowed Robert to become one of Canterbury's most respected legal minds. Robert, and his wife Jane, completed the ten some in attendance this day at Broome Park.

The Bridal Party began their celebrating in London two days ago and continued it in the 2 carriage rides to County Kent, where they were looking to finalize the celebration at the Oxenden Home. The Ladies would gather to discuss Elizabeth's new duties, and the Men were looking forward to "Shooting" and "Cigars", as all were happy that Henry had found a love to replace Charlotte, whom he missed greatly for the five years since her passing. Someone was needed to not just be a companion for the 8th Baronet, but also to help rear his four children by Charlotte. It was those duties, that most scared the new bride.

But, today, was not to think of children, but of her new husband and their family and their friends. Elizabeth had come to know Henry's emotions and sensed his concern over the intruder at the Employee Party on the front lawn, and she wondered just how he would handle this situation. Calming her hand as they stepped back into the parlor, Henry let his guests know, "Nothing to concern ourselves about right now, my friends," Henry, as he grabbed a glass from the sidebar table, under the west window, lifted it high and said, "Thank you all for coming. We shall have great fun the next few days, and please toast with me; to my beautiful wife, Elizabeth. May her beauty blind me forever!"

"Here, here!" came the reply from all 8 guests.

Back in the Stockade, as I lay on the bed of hay, I pondered my approach to explain to Sir Henry, my reasons for "happening" on to Broome Park. As the entire property was more than just a home; it also served as a community for its' people, who worked the land. Before going into the jail, I had noticed numerous buildings in this small enclave. Buildings for a Blacksmith, a grocery, complete with vegetable stand in front, assorted shops, and a Church in the center of things, served as a reminder that the Church of England extended into each and every community. A couple dozen other edifices likely served as homes to those who work, either in the small village, or for the Oxenden Family, rearing the livestock and produce.

Those who worked within the Broome Park home likely had their own apartments in the lower floor, while extra help for events such as would be needed this weekend with ten house guests, were probably villagers, who had regular "estate jobs", but pitched in at the home for special occasions.

Knowing that it was likely, that I would eventually be brought into the house to converse with Sir Henry, I began trying to imagine what the inside would look like. Our guest room was perhaps still the same as Lisa and I experienced, but what would the first floor look like. If indeed, as the outdoor celebration had indicated, that the Bridal Party had just returned from London and the Wedding, the home would be at its' palatial best. Although, I had only watched but a few episodes of Downton Abbey on television, I was guessing the Oxendens, their Guests and the attending Servants would act as those in the PBS TV Series. I could hardly wait.

No sooner than completing those thoughts, there came a hard knock at the stockade door, as I heard the jingling of keys opening the door. Two hardy souls quickly entered my quarters, and ordered me, "Stand Up You."

Having been laying there for the past half hour, my ability to quickly get up was diminished by my jailers, as they grabbed a hold of me, and began to frisk my body.

"Can I help you gentlemen?" came my reply.

"Shut up and turn around." Was the next comment, as they continued to touch me.

"He is clean of weapons." As they pushed me onto the hay, turned and exited the room and relocked the door.

Thinking to myself, "Well, wasn't that a nice

how do you do." I stood again, and went to the small slot of a window, to see if I could get a glimpse of the two visitors. However, the window did not look directly at the Big House, but rather, westwards towards the setting sun. No sooner had I stopped looking out the window, than I hear footsteps coming towards the door, and again keys where placed into the lock.

Taking a step back, as the door opened, the previous two were again coming inside. "Put your hands behind you", they said as they began to use rope to tie my hands. "The Master will see you now, and you'll be lucky if he doesn't have you whipped for trespassing." So off we went, arm in arms, as we covered the couple hundred yards from the village stockade to the back entrance of the house. As we approached, I could see several of the servants looking outside the windows at my arrival. Then, as we entered, I was told to "Sit there!" on a stool in what appeared to be part of the kitchen.

Feeling like a "dunce" in elementary school, the busy servants walked back and forth, doing their work, while glancing at the "intruder", wondering what my fate would become at the hands of the Baronet. Actually, I was marveling at the kitchen itself, working at a frenzy, as all were preparing the evening's dinner. After hearing a cart pull alongside the door to the kitchen entrance, I saw two young boys, evidently from the village, walking in carrying bushels of food. First apples, then greens, carrots and assorted vegetables which I had not ever seen before now. Male servants took the bushels from the boys and placed them into cabinets, which, when opened, emitted clouds of mist. Could these cabinets have ice in them? Was there an early version of refrigeration with which I was not familiar. In any case, ice or not, the vegetables appeared to have "cool" storage lockers.

Ladies in aprons retrieved the food, and began setting them on tables of preparation, all looking very military like in the attack on getting dinner ready for the Baronet and his guests. On the other side of the kitchen, some 30 feet away from my stool, was an open hearth fireplace, already ablaze, looking like some dozen or so wooden logs, would provide the necessary heat to cook the pheasant that lay on another table, adjacent to the fire pit.

All in all, I was impressed that a dozen or so servants each knew what he or she was to do for tonight's dinner, and just as I was feeling like a comfortable visitor, allowed to view the busy kitchen, in walked Mr. Reeves, neatly dressed in a tuxedo. He had the look of someone in charge, but in my case, I felt he was merely the constable taking me to the judge for my trial.

I rose to my feet as he approached. He looked sternly into my eyes, and stated, "His Lordship is in a wonderful mood, for your sake, and that of his guests, I suggest you be as honest as you can with his line of questioning. Please follow me." Reeves turned and walked down a hall towards the front of the house. As we exited the kitchen, we came upon the wide staircase, which Lisa and I encountered, when we took our self-guided tour, earlier this day. I mean this day in 2022. Reeves led me to the left side of the staircase and down a hallway, past several closed doors, until we came upon, what looked to be a library. As I walked in, I noticed many shelves, loaded with leather bound editions of everything ranging from Law Books, to a shelf that contained a book, written by Charles Dickens. Sir Henry's newest addition to his library, if I remember anything about the timing of Dickens' literary career, meant that this book had just recently been written and printed, and here it was in Broome Park's Library.

"Sit here", commanded Reeves.

I obeyed. Sitting there, I continued to notice the surroundings, and saw a shelf of newspapers. Upon closer examination, they were documents which featured the notation atop each page, "Official Summary of Parliament – August 5, 1848." I remembered from my conversations with Uncle Pat, that Sir Henry's Grandfather, was a Member of Parliament, but I was curious, as to this Baronet's possession of such records. Perhaps all aristocracy was supplied with the minutes of Parliament, so all were abreast of the Government's activities. In any case, with each passing second, I was becoming more impressed with the Oxenden Family's connection to those in power in London.

I then heard footsteps coming down the hallway, and they slowed in pace, as they came near the library entrance. Dressed in, what I guessed was formal evening attire, stood Sir Henry. He said nothing as he entered and walked behind his desk, and again looked me over from head to toe. He then turned towards Reeves as he sat in his chair and simultaneously withdrew a pistol from his top right hand desk drawer, while saying, "Thank you Reeves. I see our guest's hands are tied and I don't anticipate any trouble, so please wait until you hear my ring for you."

"Are you sure, my Lord?" came Reeves reply, obviously concerned about his Master being alone with an unknown person.

"Thanks for your concern Reeves, but," looking at me directly, "You don't plan on causing any problems for us, do you my friend?"

"No sir. Absolutely not." Came my answer.

"Good." Replied Henry, as he waved Reeves out the door. He walked over to the door, pistol in hand and gently closed the door. I somehow suspected, Reeves didn't go very far, for fear his Lordship, might have trouble with me.

"Now then. As it was explained to me by Reeves and a few other Servants who were at today's festivities down by the village, you decided to come on my property and walked up to where everyone was celebrating on the back lawn of the estate. Is that correct?" asked Henry.

"Yes sir." I replied, now realizing my fate might just lie with this encounter. I tried to think of how best to explain to him, when and why I came here.

"May I ask you, why you were so bold as to

come on private property without an invitation?" He said as he once again sat down at his desk.

"I also would like to know, from where you were coming and to where are you going? And in addition, your English dialect is not familiar to me, and yet normally, I can place an individual by the way they sound, within 30 minutes of where they were born. Your voice is totally strange to me." He added.

"Sir Henry. May I call you Sir Henry?" I asked. He nodded and I continued. "Sir Henry, I'm not sure how to explain all of this to you, because I am not sure you will believe me."

"Explain away." He gestured, as he sat more upright in his chair. "But, before you do, please explain to me your footwear. I find them most fascinating, as I also do with the rest of your attire. Your clothes are not shabby, so you don't appear to be a beggar, but your clothes are not of style, so as to lead me to believe, you are a person of some means."

"Perhaps Sir Henry, if you will allow me, I would like to tell you a story." I paused, as I looked for his approval to continue with my strategy of explanation. He again nodded, so I began; "I have an Uncle Patrick, who loved to share with me, aspects of history, especially English history. He did research on our family, and found that, believe it or not, we have a slight connection to Broome Park." I paused again to gauge his reaction.

"So, you are here to claim your rights as a descendant of the Oxendens?" He proposed.

"No Sir, not at all." I replied in as calm a voice as possible. "Although there is no blood relation to you, there is a blood connection, with your new wife, Elizabeth Phoebe."

Standing up and holding the pistol tightly, he walked around the desk and right up to my chair. "There is a law in the country, that any landowner has the right and duty, to protect his property and family from anyone that trespasses. What this means is, that I have every right to pull this trigger, and our conversation, and your life, will both end simultaneously." He stood there defiantly awaiting my reply.

"Sir Henry, I know that only too well. I knew the moment I stepped on to your land, that I ran that very risk. However, I also know a lot about you, and your family, and I believe you are not the type of person who would take the step of ending someone's life, without wanting to know more about why I came here."

"Virtually every citizen of County Kent, knows a great deal about the Oxenden Family. What is so special about your knowing about my family." He said, as he walked backwards and sat down on the front side of his desk.

"Because, I know, not just about you and the 7 Baronets that came before you, I also know about the two Baronets that will follow you." I spoke and then awaited his response.

"What do you mean two Baronets? You likely know of my eldest son, who will become the 9th Baronet. But a 10th? Are you implying something devious?" He said.

"Not at all. I not only know about the Oxenden's and the Dean's and the Dixwell's and the last 500 plus years of your family, I also know about the next 70 years of your family." I awaited a reply, but none came, so I continued. "Let me tell you that I'm not a soothsayer, nor a spirit, nor a prophet, nor anything else out of the ordinary. However, I am distantly, very distantly, related to your new wife, Elizabeth Phoebe Tanner."

"By the way, you haven't told me your name." He demanded.

"My name is Evan Christian. My Uncle's name

is Patrick Tanner. And he is a 5-time descendent Nephew of Elizabeth." I stated.

"Now, you're talking in riddles, and I am not in the mood for riddles." He turned, rang for Reeves, who appeared at the door, within seconds. "Reeves, this, Mr. Evan Christian, is going to spend the night in our jail. I have guests, with whom I should be, and for now, I do not have time for this charlatan tonight. Please arrange for him to have a meal and a blanket for sleep, and I will summon him, after our guests leave tomorrow afternoon. Please see no harm comes to him." Henry turned towards Reeves, giving him the pistol, and walked out the door.

Standing over me, like a jailer, Reeves then said, "In my 20 years of service to my Lordship, I have never seen him as upset as he is now. I suggest you spend tonight praying as, when the guests leave, you will likely need it." Reeves now motioned me, with the pistol, out the door and down the hall, from where we came. Entering the kitchen, once again, I drew stares and the sight of the pistol in the hand of Reeves, caused a few gasps. As we exited the back of the house, the two men who led me to the house from jail, were motioned by Reeves, to come forward.

"Gentlemen," said Reeves, "Please gently escort our intruder back to the stockade. Please see to it that he gets the meal, which I will arrange to be delivered to the jail, for him. I will also send a blanket for his use tonight."

Surprisingly, not a word was said by my two escorts, until they opened the jail door. "Good luck to you tomorrow mate. His Grace is known for his kindness, but I dare say, he never has liked trespassers."

With that, they closed the door and once again, I was alone. I began to think of Lisa, wondering if my desire to find more answers, would prevent me from ever seeing her again. What would Sir Henry want of me tomorrow? As I reviewed the words I said to him in the library, I knew, whatever I next said to him, would need to have more conciseness to it. My rambling thoughts today, I think, only frustrated my host, and that alone, was not good for my situation. His patience might be limited, knowing I've somewhat spoiled his return home, following the wedding. Would he share my comments with Elizabeth, about my Uncle being her nephew? That alone would be confusing enough to scare her, and getting her on my side, I felt, was key to my strategy.

I started to think of the family tree which Uncle Patrick had shared with me several years ago. Elizabeth's Father and Mother, James and Sarah, were born in 1790 and 1795. Why I remember those dates exactly, was beyond me. I just envisioned the family tree, which my cousin Andrew had developed for his 7th Grade Civics Class in Junior High School, some 25 years or so before now. Elizabeth's brother, James Benjamin Tanner, was born 5 years after Elizabeth, and at this point in 1848, he would be 23 years old, and already married to Mary Emma Holmes, who in that same year, had likely, already delivered her first child, Robert Tanner, who would be Elizabeth's first nephew. My claim of Uncle Pat also being a nephew would certainly cause her concern for the sanity of this visitor to Broome Park. Frederick, my own Mother's Great Grandfather, would not be alive for 3 more years, and a 3rd nephew, Edward James Tanner, would not be born until 1864, at which point, his mother, Elizabeth's Sister-in-Law, would die giving birth. Elizabeth's own sister, Mary Ann Tanner, had yet married John Griffiths. Those two would provide a home for yet to born, Frederick and Edward, after their Father's death in 1870. It was amazing to me that all this family history was coming to my mind. I somehow felt I would need all the information possible tomorrow at my next encounter with Sir Henry.

Now I needed the book. The book. (Now I know why Uncle Patrick, made a copy of one page from this book and suggested that I keep it with me, if I ever happened on Broome Park.) Reaching inside my front pocket, I took out a simple piece of paper, which contained the text from the Funeral Tablet of the Sir Henry Chudleigh's Fathers' Funeral. This book was written by Sir Henry's Fathers', lifelong Stewart, who in the book, never gave his name. Rather, he gave his manuscript to two barristers, and close friends of the 7th Baronet, Robert Collard and Edward Gibbons, who arranged for the books' publication. The book itself wasn't to be written until 24 years after the 7th Baronet's death in 1838, which wasn't printed until 14 years after this visit to Broome Park.

The Book about the 7th Baronet, was called, *Recollections of the Late, Sir Henry Oxenden, Baronet.* This, however, would not mean much to the 8th Baronet, Sir Henry Chudleigh Oxenden, except when I inform him that on the inside of the front cover of the book, his name has been placed on a placard, and stuck inside the book. Obviously, this was intended to be a gift, from the Steward, to the 8th Baronet. Possibly, the only thing which I can convey to Broome Park's current owner, is that the last page (#85) of this book, has text from the:

COPY OF THE TABLET IN BARHAM CHURCH

To the Memory of Sir Henry Oxenden,
Baronet of Broome, in this Parish.
This Tablet is raised by his Sons and Daughters,
who bear in mind his affectionate kindness and
that singular benevolence of heart, which won for
him, the love of the Poor and the esteem and
regard for all.
He died peacefully, Sept. 22nd, 1838,
Aged 82 years.
And near him, in the adjoining vault, repose
the remains of his beloved Wife,
Mary Lady Oxenden.
The hoary head is a crown of glory, if it be
found in the way of righteousness."
Proverbs 16, verse 31.

Re-folding this piece of paper, I placed it back into my front pocket, as I predict I will need it at my next encounter with Sir Henry. Still, how can I explain that I got it from my Uncle Patrick. Sir Henry would rather think that I recently had visited Barham Church and chose to write down the words on this piece of paper. The key? How can Sir Henry explain why this simple piece of paper, with "blue lines" and "spiral holes" on it. Sir Henry may know about Lined Paper, as it was in 1770, that Englishman, John Tellow was issued the first patent for manufactured, lined paper. But it wasn't until 1934 that the USA Patent Office, issued a patent for the spiral paper notebook. Thank goodness I did my homework on this little piece of paper, given to me by Uncle Pat. Did my Uncle know that it would be of critical importance to me at some point in the future; or more correctly, at some point in the past?

In any case, suddenly, I realized just how I would present, "my defense for trespassing" to Sir Henry. How he would react to that defense, I could not be sure of, but at least I now felt a calmness come over me. I was going to be OK.

Just then, the jail door keys, were placed in the lock, and it soon opened, with 3 people entering. They were my two "jailor companions", and one "Kitchen Maid" whom I remember seeing, in my two walks through Broome Park's Kitchen.

"With compliments of His Grace, Sir Henry, here is your dinner sir," She stated, as she set the tray down on the 2 foot high tree stump, which obviously served the jail's occupants, as both a stool and in this case, as a table. From under the tray, she also pulled out a folded blanket. Although, this didn't appear to be a very luxurious blanket, it was made of wool, and would be much appreciated, should tonight's temperatures dip into the 40's.

"Please convey my thanks to Sir Henry." I politely accepted this hospitality.

With that, the three exited my quarters, and re-locked the door, as I heard their footsteps going away. Looking underneath the bowl cover, the aroma was wonderful, as it looked like a bowl of clam chowder complete with croutons. Picking up the accompanying spoon, I dipped it into the bowl, and slowly tasted the mixture; it was Clam Chowder! Not as potato filled as a New England version, but nonetheless, this soup contained several clams, that I am guessing were caught recently in the Channel, at nearby Dover.

Along with the soup, my tray had two pieces of freshly made bread, still warm from the oven. Although, I was not invited to Sir Henry and Lady Elizabeth's Homecoming Dinner, I am guessing that this was to be their first course for tonight's meal. Whomever the cook was, he or she, did a fantastic job, as in all my travels, I've not tasted any better chowder. What a delight.

After emptying my bowl, the breadbasket and the stoneware mug, which contained, of all things, beer! I managed to make myself comfortable as the time of day, I guessed, was approaching the setting of the sun. I was correct, as within minutes after laying down, the last rays of sunshine stopped coming through the small cracks, between the logs of my stockade. For late August, at this parallel, I estimated it was about 9:00pm in the evening, as day light savings time, would not be in use, worldwide for another 50 years or so.

Recounting the last two days' activities brought a smile to my face. From leaving Heathrow, and relinquishing our two seats back to home, Lisa and I drove Britain's motorways around London, to Canterbury and Broome Park. Followed by an early morning rise to play golf in hopes of getting lost in the fog, to immediately finding myself in 1848, and actually meeting the new husband of my five-time Great Aunt, to being in jail, was quite a journey. I only hoped my saga would return me safe and sound to Lisa and our

Children. I was determined not to worry about that issue, and I quickly fell fast asleep.

Meanwhile, back inside Broome Park's Dining Hall, I assumed the Wedding Celebration continued. Unbeknownst to me, Clam Chowder was indeed the evening's first course, followed by Pheasant, Lamb, Beef, all grown on the rolling hills of the Estate's 5,000 acres, and as it had been for the last 33 years, was prepared under the joint guidance of Reeves and Head Housekeeper, Phoebe Norris, both of whom had worked for Sir Henry's Father. Henry and Elizabeth's guests reveled in the bounty provided them, with Henry and Priscilla Carnarvon, of Highclere Castle, commenting that their own Kitchen could not surpass what Broome Park's Staff had prepared for them tonight. That indeed was a compliment that thrilled Sir Henry, as he truly wanted his beloved Elizabeth to treasure her new home and its' surroundings.

With those wonderful compliments, Lady Elizabeth, leaned over to her husband of less than one week, and gently kissed him on the cheek, as she whispered, "Thank you my love for bringing me to your paradise." The 8th Baronet could hardly contain his pride in the Family Estate and replied humbly, "Thank you kind guests. The true measure of Broome Park is our wonderful staff, whose members have been serving us for generations. My Father in particular, would want to say thank you as well."

"Here, here!" came the reply as all in the dining hall lifted their glasses to the Oxenden's of Past and Present. The partying lasted well into the evening, and eventually, the equally long day for the Owner and Guests came to an end, as each was escorted to their bedrooms for a well-deserved rest.

CHAPTER 13

WHAT WOULD TODAY BRING?

The morning sunshine came early, as it seeped through the east side crevices of my lodging room. All it took was one ray to meet my eyelid, as its' strength and warmth triggered my consciousness to start another day.

Yawning and stretching came easily this morning, as I was surprised at the restful sleep which I had just enjoyed. Heaven knows I needed the rest and heaven also was the only one that knew how the days' events would play out for themselves. Outside the jail I heard a myriad of activity, and as I stood to peak out the small crack of a window facing east and towards the main path of the village buildings, a dozen or so people were already busy with their jobs. I could smell the bakery, even though I couldn't tell from which building the aroma originated. I also heard, what sounded like a blacksmith's hammer on the anvil, as something made of steel was being pounded into form for some use in another of the village's edifices.

The play of little children could also be heard, as I was wondering, "Did English Servant Children, have Summer Vacations? Did they even have schools for them, this far away from London or Canterbury? If so, which village resident was the schoolmaster? Was it a woman? Likely not. More probable was that these children were either home schooled, or had no schooling at all, or occasionally a visiting teacher would frequent the estate, giving lesson material to those under age 12, likely at the request of the Baronets.

Would they have encouraged the education of those who served them? Reeves was as polished as any servant could possibly become. It is likely that all the servants at Broome Park or Highcleer or Leeds Castle or at any of the Aristocracy's numerous estates would, at least, be educated in extremely good manners, and those in management of other workers, would have a knowledge of local and worldly customs and events, so as to reflect an atmosphere of excellence throughout the entire staff of workers, most particularly, the staff that had household duties. Those field workers would of course be trained in etiquette, but further education expectations would be limited to the opportunities which likely didn't avail themselves to too many individuals not from a certain level of society.

Nonetheless, an enterprise the size of Broome Park would require great organizational skills from the owner to the house managers to the field foreman to ensure the grounds developed the needed "produce and livestock" which would help pay the expenses of this unincorporated corporation. For it to last for generations is proof alone that whatever they did, it worked. Did the servitude of their employees amount to tantamount slavery? Remembering the text from Sir Henry the 7th's biographical tribute book, the financial production of Broome Park was marvelous. The loving and caring of the people who served the Oxenden family was one of a truly effective caretaker of land and people.

As the book listed those servants, it also listed their years of service, and literally there were several dozen employees who worked for the family for 40+ years and more. Why not. Working hard, as I'm sure it was for each of the estate's disciplines, not only provided employment and lodging to those workers, but security within the boundaries of Broome Park. Venturing to the outside world, other than occasional trips to London, Canterbury or Dover, those who did might come across highwaymen, or others of ill-repute who might do harm to anyone who found themselves without the security provided by the comfort of Broome Park.

I wondered if, because of my intrusion on to their environment, if those workers were wondering about the fate I would have today. They all had to be told that the "stranger" spent the night in the stockade, awaiting Sir Henry's attention, once his house guests would be departing today. Normally, guests coming this far would stay for days, do some hunting and shooting, as well as, partying, but evidently, because they had already been celebrating for 72 hours, they likely were returning to all their own homes. I'd find out soon.

The next several hours passed slowly. I could still hear and peek through cracks to see what was happening in the village, and I heard noise to the South, towards the house, but couldn't see anything to determine if Sir Henry's guests were gone, or still in Broome Park. Eventually, I noticed that today lacked sunshine. I couldn't make out if there was any fog, and wondered if that would play a role with me later. Then, I heard footsteps, coming towards the jail at a fairly brisk pace. As well, I heard others murmuring to each other, and numerous other footsteps. Was Sir Henry summoning me and were the villagers coming closer to the stockade out of curiosity?

The steps stopped. Then, a pounding on the door, proceeded the keys entering the lock and the door opening. In walked the same two from yesterday. As they stepped inside, the smaller one stated, "Evan Christian arise and follow me, as Sir Henry is ready to deal with you." I had been sitting on the stump but stood quickly. They retied my hands with rope, which they had untied when they dropped me here last night.

As I was exiting the door, the same kitchen maid passed by me into the jail. I guess to retrieve the tray and dishes. I turned towards her to and said, "Thank you Miss for last night's food. It was very tasty."

"Never mind your food, keep walking." Said the tall one. As we continued, I remembered several of the faces on the villagers from the lawn party yesterday, including the face of the aggressive maiden, who started the chaos that led to Reeves confronting me. She smiled at me and waved, as though I was some kind of sports hero going into the arena.

Within a minute or so, we, once again, entered the kitchen, where I was met by Reeves. "I trust, Mr. Christian, that you had a restful night?"

"I did Reeves. Thank you kindly and for the nice meal as well." I replied.

"Would you like anything to eat right now?" Reeves stated as he anticipated my hunger, as the soup, bread and beer, were the only food I'd had in some time.

"I would love some, please." I responded with enthusiasm.

"Here you go, sir." Came the soft voice from one of the kitchen maids, who handed me a bowl, of what appeared to be oatmeal. "It is porridge sir. Good English porridge." She added. "And, here is some tea as well."

"Thank you kindly. You are all very kind." I said with as much sincerity as possible as I sat down at the kitchen's table. Reeves untied my hands.

It didn't take but a few minutes for me to eat the meal, and the timing was perfect as it calmed my nervous stomach for my forthcoming meeting with Sir Henry. The staff looked to be as busy as last night, and it looked like they were preparing another hearty meal for the Lord and Lady of the house.

I turned towards Reeves, who stood motionless only a few feet from my eating table. "Mr. Reeves, have Sir Henry's guests left Broome Park?"

"Never you mind about that. Your issue is with Sir Henry." Came the stern reply. "OK now," Reeves said, as I finished my meal. "Come with me."

"By the way, Mr. Reeves," I said, as I rose from the table. "Please tell me the time."

"The time?" He inquired. He pulled out his pocket watch, which was chain tied to his pocket and glanced down, and then back at me. "Precisely, 5:00 pm." He said, placing the watch back into his pocket and giving me a puzzled look, as to why I had asked the question.

"Thank you, Reeves," I said, as I reached into my back pants pocket to retrieve my own wristwatch, which I had taken off upon entering Broome Park's property line, so as not to cause undo questions. Actually, I knew that wristwatches had been around England for years. However, they were mostly worn by women, as they were considered more of a bracelet, than a watch. In the mid-19th Century, men, like Reeves, used pocket watches exclusively, so I wasn't surprised at his reaction to my placing the watch over my wrist, and snapping it into place.

"You wear a bracelet, Mr. Christian?" He asked indignantly.

"Why yes Reeves, from where I come, both Men and Women wear them." I replied.

"Yours is rather any interesting design, I must say." He said, as he studied my arm, which I extended for him to get a better look at the watch.

"Where is it, exactly, that you live?" He inquired, as he motioned me down the same hallway as last night.

"As much as I would love to tell you Reeves, I think I should let Sir Henry know first. Don't you think?" I asked.

"You are probably correct Mr. Christian." Reeves agreed, as we got to Sir Henry's same study room as last night. "Please enter and sit there." He said, pointing to the same chair I had occupied before. Then, Reeves stood motionless, as I assumed, we were both awaiting Sir Henry's entrance.

Walking through the door, at a brisk pace, Sir Henry began with, "And did our guest have a good night's sleep in our stockade?" He continued around the table into his chair.

"I did Sir Henry. And I thank you for the meal then and just now." I said.

"Yes, of course. It's nearly supper time, and your breakfast was a little behind schedule I'd say." He smiled, seeming to be in a better mood than when we last met.

"I'm being treated more that fairly, Sir." I offered.

"That is good. Prisoner, patron or host, we must all eat, don't you think so Reeves." He said, turning to the Butler to include him in the conversation.

"Quite right sir." Reeves replied. "It appears our guest is a man of mystery, but tending one's appetite, is needed by all, Sir."

"A Man of Mystery is quite the right way to put it Reeves. I think I will spend some more time, alone, with our Guest." Henry stated, again turning towards Reeves, as his sign for Reeves to exit and close the door.

"As you wish, Sir. Please ring if you need me." Responded Reeves, exiting the room.

The room was silent for several seconds, but to me, it seemed much longer. "Well, Mr. Christian. I must apologize for my seeming loss of temperament last night. I should have waited until my guests had been fed before we met." He explained as he sat back in his desk chair, and he appeared to be much more relaxed today.

"That is understandable Sir Henry." I said. "I too, am more relaxed. "I trust, your dinner last night with your house guests went well for all."

Surprised by my inquiry, he replied, "It did. Last night did go well. It did go well. Once, we began dinner, I thought only of them and their enjoyment. Thank you."

"Are they still with you Sir Henry?" I asked.

"No. Well most have gone. Only Elizabeth's sister, Mary Tanner, and her companion, Robert Trentworthy have stayed on for a few more days. The Earl had to get back to London, so, we postposed the Hunting until next time." He pondered as he replied. "However, this morning, I did share with Elizabeth your claim as a relation to her, and she was puzzled with the claim of your Uncle Patrick being her nephew. I intend to ask her in here after we have talked a little more. So, let's return to our conversation of last night. Just, who are you? From where do you come? Where are you headed? And, why, did you come to Broome Park?" Completing his questioning, he then sat back to hear my reply.

"When we talked last night, you made the statement that I was talking in riddles and what I was saying obviously upset you, and rightly so. For someone of my age…." I began only to be interrupted by Henry.

"Exactly how old are you?" He insisted.

"I just turned 53 years old this month." I said.

"Fifty-three? I am…" He began to say.

"Fifty-three." I said. Then, we starred at each other for a moment.

"You are correct. I am 53." He said with interest. "But you look much younger than I. You look more like you are in your late 30's." He stated.

"There is a reason for all this, which I hope to share further with you." I replied, as he was now showing genuine interest in every word I spoke.

"Continue." As he waved his hand in a forward motion. "Continue."

"Let me put it another way for you." I began my explanation. "My Father, David Christian, will not be born until 100 years from this summer." I stopped and waited for a response, but his reaction was of continued silence, but intense attention. "I then came along 21 years later. You see, Sir Henry, I am from the future. I know this must be hard for you to comprehend, and I must confess, equal difficulty, that I am where I am at this moment."

Slowly, he rose and began walking around the room, in a puzzled state. "But how? Where? Who? Why?" He mumbled. Then, his eyes lit up. "I am guessing that you are an American; aren't you?" He turned with intense focus on me.

"I am. And I was on Vacation, or should I say, on Holiday. My wife, Lisa, and I had been touring England and Scotland for 38 days, when we came to County Kent for our last two days. We came at the suggestion of my Uncle Patrick.....Tanner." I paused to see if he had a question.

"Tanner? Then... Elizabeth....and Mary are both your Great Aunts." He realized. "But, how? How did you get to 1848?" He asked.

"Believe me when I say that part was not planned." I explained. "You see, several years ago, before my Uncle Patrick disappeared, he shared a great deal with me, about our family history and specifically, a lot about Broome Park and the Oxendens."

"What do you mean disappeared? Did he die?" Asked Henry.

"We assume he is dead, but we never found out. We only know that he and his wife, my Aunt Marilyn, were on holiday in Switzerland, when they were reported missing. They were never found." I paused to catch my own breath.

Henry had the look that a thousand questions were going around in his mind, and he needed to sort which one to next ask. "But, but….what did he tell you about us, me, …..Elizabeth?" He asked.

"After he just shared with me all he could, Uncle Patrick just asked that the next time we come to England, make sure you go to County Kent and Broome Park." I explained.

"We? You mean you and your wife?" He asked and I nodded. "Well, where is she right now?"

"This you find hard the hardest to believe. Right now, my wife, Lisa, is here in Broome Park.

Only she is not here in 1848. We rented the room on the 3rd floor, front left, facing your garden building that sits in front of your pond behind it. She is sitting there, only in the year 2022." I stated and then kept silent.

"2022?" He said. The look on his face reminded me of the look on Jimmy Stewart's face in the movie "It's a Wonderful Life", just after the Angel, Clarence, told him, he had never been born.

"I know this must be hard for you to understand, but…" I started.

"Ridiculous. You're nothing but a charlatan, just like I said last night. You are tricking me. What is it that you are after? You will get no money from me." He stood and glared at me, trying to rationalize his disbelief.

"If I may Sir Henry. I'd like to show you something. May I?" I asked.

"Yes. Yes. Go ahead." He said. Waving his hand in approval.

I stood up and reached into my front pocket and pulled out the piece of paper I reviewed last night in jail. As I unfolded the paper, I reached forward with it, giving it to Henry. Slowly, he grabbed it, looking at me at the same time. As he took it, he examined the paper on both sides, running his hand over the torn edges of the spiral portion of the paper, which he obviously could not understand the torn edges. Then, he began to read it, and slowly sat back down in his chair.

"How? Where did you get this? You must have just come from Barham Church and copied this down." He explained with his reasoning.

"How do you explain the blue lines on the paper?" I asked.

Again, he examined the paper, and was silent, thinking of his reply. Then, he reached into his desk drawer and took out a short stack of paper and plopped it on to the top of his desk. "Lined paper. This is not unusual for people in my position to obtain. Here are some Parliamentary communications written on lined paper." He stated.

"What about the torn holes on the paper. This paper is from a "spiral notebook", and I tore out the pages." I explained.

"Spiral Notebook?" He asked.

"It won't be invented until sometime in the 20th century in the United States of America. There will be many inventions in the coming 100 years. Many from America, and many from Great

Britain. It will be a fascinating time. Later they will name this period in time, "The Industrial Revolution!" I offered. "Already in Wales, you have Coal Mines, that will help make Britain stronger as a Trading Country, supplying Coal and other goods to other countries around the world. In America, we call ourselves, the USA and like England, the USA will develop inventions that will stagger the world's imagination." I continued.

Trying to digest my comments, he then looked down again at the paper and asked, "What has this got to do with you coming here?" He asked.

"I didn't really know until I got here in England." I said, as it was dawning on me, how to go further with my explanation. "As I stated, my Uncle Patrick wrote this down and gave it to me. I brought it with me to England, because when in County Kent, I thought having this and going to Barham Church, and seeing it on the church wall, it would tie my whole trip together."

"Then, you did just come from Barham Church." Henry stated.

"No. I never got there. It was only when I was at Heathrow Airport, planning to return to Broome Park, that I took it from my briefcase and

placed it into my pocket, in case I would need it."
I said.

"What and where is Heathrow Air...?" He
inquired.

I tried not to laugh, but the shear uniqueness
of the question, caused me to smile broadly.
"Remember me talking about the numerous
inventions that would occur in the next 100
years?" I said as he looked and nodded. "Well,
probably one of the most significant was the
airplane." I paused to see if he had a question.
He shook his head but said nothing. "Fifty-five
years from now, on December 19, 1903, in the
American state of North Carolina, in the ocean
town of Kitty Hawk, two brothers name Orville
and Wilbur Wright, who make bicycles for a
living, will pilot a vehicle that can fly." Looking
at Henry's stunned look, I continued. "Yes, one of
them actually flew the contraption into the air for
about 500 meters. The invention was eventually
called an aeroplane or airplane. And England will
have numerous places around the country where
these airplanes will take off into the sky and fly
from place to place and land at other air....ports."
I again paused to gauge Henry's absorption of my
statements, but he sat motionless but attentive,

so I continued. "England's Heathrow Airport, is one of the largest in the world, and it takes up as much land as the whole acreage of Broome Park."

"Why so large?" Asked Henry.

"The Wright Brothers invention only had one passenger on it; Orville. But, as inventions evolve, other companies began to make similar aircraft and new aircraft was developed that would carry "passengers", who would ride along in the plane, which would be "piloted" or driven, by trained pilots.

"Passengers? You mean like how we drove down from London after the wedding in two carriages?" Asked Henry. "What makes this aeroplane fly?" He added.

"What helps it to fly is another invention; the internal combustion engine, which will be created by the German inventor, Hans VanOhazn around the year 1863. Then a second inventor, an Englishman named Frank Whittle, will be born 59 years from now. He will enhance VanOhazn's engine, calling it a Turbo Jet Engine with power enough to launch into the air, an airplane that weighs thousands of pounds, including the weight of as many as 300 passengers." I paused as Sir Henry attempted to digest all this information.

I continued, "A great amount of land is needed, so that "runways" can be built out of concrete. These cement runways are roads that will be a mile long or longer, as it takes a while for the aircraft to gain speed provided by the engine, before the aeroplanes' "wings", act just like a gliding birds' wings lift that bird skyward."

At this point, Henry began to smile and to seem less amazed, "You know Mr. Christian, that my Father would not have been as surprised as I have acted, about all your statements."

I replied, "From what I know about the 7th Baronet, he seemed like a great man. I'm sorry you lost him in 1838."

"You know that from this piece of paper and the text at Barham Church?" He confirmed.

"I know it from a wonderful book, which was written about your father." I stated.

"A book about my Father? When was it written? Who wrote it?" He begged.

"It hasn't been written yet. Not for another couple of years, and I am sorry to say, that the Author remained anonymous, yet I do know it was one of your Father's Stewards." I stated.

"Robert Smith!" He stated and asked simultaneously.

"No, but Mr. Smith's 50 years of service to your father is duly noted in the book. My Uncle Pat was in possession of a copy of the book. You will read it in the coming years." I added.

"I, in coming years? You know how long I will live? Please tell me. No, no do not tell me." He paused as I could tell he wanted to know his future, but he also did not want to know. "What about my Elizabeth? No, please don't tell me, I couldn't stand knowing when I would lose her. Not after losing Charlotte." He paused again. "You know of Charlotte?"

"I do, Sir Henry, and I am so sorry about your losing her at so young an age. There are things for you to know and many more things for you and your family to discover. I will only offer this statistic. You, Sir Henry, will live longer than any other Oxenden Baronet has ever lived. I tell you this, not to spoil the future for you or to make you anxious about the future, but rather, now that I have gotten to know the history of Broome Park and your Families, especially, your Father, who I know from his biography, that he was an incredibly kind man, benevolent beyond belief. You must have had a wonderful upbringing Sir Henry." I finished, for the moment.

"He was. He was kind. I miss him." Turning to me, with almost tears in his eyes, he continued, "Evan, I cannot begin to tell you how much I appreciate your coming here. I'm not sure how you got here. Wait. How did you get here and how will you get back to your time in the future?" He inquired.

"For lack of a better explanation, let's call my coming here, Time Travel." I stated. "Moving through time, is unexplainable, but I'm here and yet, so is my wife Lisa. She is likely sitting in our sleeping room or walking through your wonderful gardens." I stated.

"It's all so bewildering. Time travel. Aeroplane travel. You and your wife being here at the same place, but in differing years. What other inventions will there be?" He started and then stopped. "Wait, I want Elizabeth to hear these things."

"Are you sure, Sir Henry? Let me explain a few more things to you." I began as Henry returned to his chair. "How I got here is unexplainable but here is what I experienced. We came to Broome Park to see what it was like. For what I am about to tell you, you can be very proud. Our visit to England in 2022, is 174 years from now. You will be happy to know that the building, your home, Broome Park, on the outside and many rooms within the home, look exactly like they did as you live in it now. The fact that this building was structured in 1638-1643, is a testament to both its' builder and your family for its' wonderful care."

"2022…. Amazing. Is it still owned by our family? There must be the 20th Baronet in charge. Is that correct?" He asked.

"Let me set aside that answer for later. For now, let me explain my arrival. As I stated before, we had left the last two days of our 40-day holiday, to visit Broome Park. When we got here, I was out for a walk, (I thought explaining the golf course and the demise of the Baronetcy was not for Henry's knowing, so a simple walk seemed the best answer). This walk took me North from the house. After about a mile northward, a tremendously thick fog, came rolling over the top of the house, and then proceeded to fall down upon me."

"Oh yes, we frequently get thick fog from the Channel, that leaves us in the dark for sometimes hours. It's a way of life in County Kent." He volunteered. "Sorry for the interruption. Please continue."

"Quite alright. You are correct. The fog was so thick and cold, that I was totally lost. I yelled and yelled to no avail, as no one could hear me. I then, began hearing voices, and they were talking about an airplane coming in for a landing." I stopped as he was going to talk.

"Airplanes? Here at Broome Park?" He asked.

"Yes, Sir Henry. I have the unfortunate truth to tell you, that in the next century, there will be two more wars. These will be World Wars, involving virtually every country. I will tell you that Great Britain and the USA become great allies in the future. Other great countries join us to stop the evil that comes out of central Europe. This happens twice. Both times the Allies win the war, but at great costs, to both Human life and the infrastructures of many countries. I hate to state that even in 2022, there is still great evil in the world, from which, the rest of the world, must work together to ward off that evil. The evil is one person or group of people, trying to dominate others." I stated.

"Sounds like Religious wars?" He asked.

"Unfortunately, some of them were. You are

correct." I responded. "To make matters worse. Some of the inventions of the future, added to the severity of war. Guns and cannons and worse have been perfected, and with the aeroplane, came the ability to take cannonballs, so to speak, on the planes and drop them on targets causing tremendous explosions and loss of life and property."

"Catapults from the sky." He pondered.

"Precisely." I replied. "During the second world war, Broome Park became a regional Allied Military operations' location and an airport was built for Allied planes to land here. Well, when I got lost in the fog in 2022, all of a sudden, I was caught in time, (between 1941 and 1944, I think), and I heard a plane crashing and people attempting to put out the ensuing fires. No sooner than hearing this, the fog began to lift, and I found myself walking back to Broome Park's house, as I was back in 2022."

"Amazing." He said.

"The amount of time I was lost in the fog, seemed to me, to be about 30 minutes, but the people of Broome Park, said I had been gone for 3-4 hours. Upon sharing this with another Broome Park visitor, a banker from London, a

Mr. Witherington, he shared with me, his similar experience from a previous summer visit here. Only he went back in time, we think, to about the 1700's. And still another individual I met, stated he went back as far as King Edward III to "only hear" people talking. None of us actually met people, like I have on this, my second visit." I stopped and took a breath.

"Would you like a drink of something?" Asked Henry. I nodded and Henry rang for Reeves, who responded in seconds and entered the room. "My dear and faithful Mr. Reeves, did I ever tell you how greatly I appreciate your loyal service over these many years? If I did not, then I am sorry, for I am truly grateful for what you have done for my family."

Acting stunned by the Baronet's openly gracious attitude, Reeves replied, "Your most welcome Sir, and you have thanked me, many times before sir."

"Then, I thank you again, my friend." Henry joyfully proclaimed. "Would you please bring Mr. Christian and me something wonderful to drink."

"Would champagne be adequate Sir." He asked.

Looking at me, I nodded and so did Henry. "Champagne it is Sir. I do also want to say, that Lady Elizabeth is curious beyond question about your discussions here. What shall I tell her Sir?"

"Tell her a few more minutes and we will come to her in the drawing room. Just a few more minutes." He stated.

"Very well Sir." Said Reeves as he closed the door.

"What a marvelous man, Reeves. He is tireless, and yet works without ever a complaint." Said Henry proudly.

"He seems a very good man." I added.

"A very good man indeed." Said Henry. Just then, the knock at the door was Reeves, already with two glasses and a bottle of Veuve Clicquot Brut, as well as a basket of biscuits for us to eat.

"Excellent Reeves. Thank you so much." Wished Henry.

"You are welcome Sir." He replied as he again exited the room.

"Getting back to your story... so, 3 of you experienced coming back in time, all to Broome Park grounds, yet none of you saw or talked WITH anyone. Is that correct?" He asked.

"Yes, Sir Henry." I said.

"Why don't we suspend you calling me Sir Henry, and just call me Henry. All right with you." He asked.

"Fine with me Henry and please, Evan for you as well." I replied.

"Good, like old friends, Evan and Henry. Please continue. What happened next?" He stated.

"After our night and day at Broome Park, we left, at the suggestion of Mr. Witherington, to go make contact, with the 3rd time traveler, a Mr. Henry Mayfield of Brighton, England." I began.

"Henry is a very popular English name. Even despite the wretchedness of the most famous Henry, the 8th." He laughed. "Brighton by the sea. A wonderful place. Used to visit there many times as a child. Please continue."

"We found the Mayfield home, and we met Henry and exchange pleasantries and he shares with us, his Broome Park Fog experience. He then provides us with a condensed, but very thorough British History lesson. Our visit was only an hour or two at most, so we thanked he and his wife, who just happens to be a Deidra Taylor by birth, which is my Grandfather Tanner's Mother's maiden name. So, it turns out, we are likely related to this Deidra Taylor, because my Grandfather

Tanner was born in Brighton on Saint Patrick's Day, 1916. He only lived in England a short time, before he, his Mother and Father and Sister, Nina, headed for Canada, living in Montreal, Toronto and Windsor, before my Grandfather, Leslie Charles Patrick Tanner, graduated from school, crossed the Detroit river into the United States, and began a 40+ year career working for a railroad company. He too loved history, as did his son, my Uncle Patrick."

"Fascinating Evan. Please keep talking." Henry insisted.

"Well, after hearing all this, we thanked the Mayfields, and headed towards Heathrow, to catch our airplane trip back to America, to Michigan, where we live." I explained.

"Michigan, is that a Province or County in America?" He asked.

"Actually, Michigan is one of 50 of the United States." I explained.

"Of course, sorry for my ignorance. I should study more about your country of we are going to become allies in the future, right?" He replied wryly.

"Definitely. The reason you may not have heard of the State of Michigan, is that at this time, 1848, the USA was growing very fast, and Michigan had just become a State in 1837. I think the number of States at that time was only 30 or so, and over the next 110 years, the total number of States will grow to 50." I said. "Anyways, as we left Brighton en route to our hotel for the night before our airplane trip across the ocean, I began to become obsessed with wanting to know more about Broome Park. I started to think that I should again try to go back in time."

"You are a born adventurer Evan." He said.

"I think that came from my Uncle Patrick." I said.

"How I wished I could meet him as well." He remarked.

"He was truly our family's historian. He loved discovering things about the family. Actually, it was through old family letters, of relatives from England, writing to my Grandfather's family, that we came across documentation, explaining that in 1848, Elizabeth Phoebe Tanner became to second wife of the 8th Baronet of Broome Park, in a wonderful wedding at St George's Church in Hanover, Westminster London. Was it a nice wedding?" I asked.

"Yes, Evan it was. I am grateful to the Lord in

Heaven for allowing me to find another Woman to again love. I was so distraught with the loss of Charlotte, as she too, was a wonderful Lady. It took me several years before I even thought of re-marriage, and then, through friends, the ones who were here today, we were introduced about a year ago and here we are today as husband and wife. I have been very blessed. And, I am blessed to have met you Evan Christian, of the Christian-Tanner America connection. How did the second visit to Broome Park occur?" He inquired.

"Well, my original plan was to place Lisa on a plane back to home, and for me to come here, to try again to get caught in the fog and go back in time." I began. "But Lisa was furious with me, fearing a might not ever return to the year 2022."

"Easily understandable." Commented Henry. "Please continue."

"The result of our argument, is that she agreed I could try again, but she would come to Broome Park with me, to wait until my return, if indeed I was able to go back into time again." I stopped to catch my breath and continued, "So, we drove here from Heathrow, in a rental car and…." Noticing Henry's puzzled look when I said the word rental car, I paused, then explained, "A car, was originally called an Automobile, which was another of the late 19th Century's inventions. A German inventor named Karl Benz, used the previously mentioned Internal Combustion Engine, and attached it to, a small carriage, which provided power to "gears" that could automatically turn the carriages back two wheels, propelling the vehicle forward."

"Amazing!" was all Henry could think of saying.

"Within a few years of this invention, other Automobile Manufacturers came into being and began providing the Wealthy people of the World, their own personal motorized transportation. However, it was an American inventor, named Henry Ford, who devised the "assembly line", which allowed cars to be mass produced, which significantly drove down the cost of these vehicles, so that many non-wealthy Americans could also utilize this wonderful invention." I continued, "Soon, England was producing vehicles as well, under the names of Rolls Royce, MGB (Motorcars of Great Britain) and Jaguar. This mode of transportation revolutionized the global economy from 1895-1925. And, to actually answer your rental car question, as people fly from one country to another, when they land

and require their own personal transportation, the "rent" an automobile for a period of time, and turn it back into the rental car company at the airport, before the "Fly home"." I paused looking at Sir Henry's reaction.

At first, he struggled for words, and mumbled a few things before composing himself and saying, "And you say that the Industrial Revolution is about to begin here in England?"

"Yes, inventors from all over Europe and America, see an invention like the Steam Engine, and used their imagination to adapt it in the production of goods, which leads to other inventions. It was a glorious time in history, which should have led to the world's prosperity, but jealous and evil minds, as there always have been, ended up using inventions to wage war on other countries, so that periodically, we still have war and the tragedies they spawn." I stopped and focused on Henry, who was in a daze trying to comprehend, all I have been stating.

"Then we should make a toast Mr. Evan Christian, to you first, for "happening" on to Broome Park, and to me for being the lucky 19th Century Person, who has received the privilege of learning about the world, ahead of time. And also, to all these inventors who will make our future world so exciting!" He stood and leaned over and clinked his champagne flute with mine.

Henry then, took a bite of a biscuit, and continued to talk, "Evan I am so glad..." he coughed as the biscuit and his champagne weren't going down his esophagus but instead his breathing tube.... He put up his hand as if to signal me he would be ok, and then smiled as though to apologize for the interruption, except that he continued to choke on his food, until he dropped his flute on his desk, and it broke.

I set down my flute and raced around the back of the desk saying, "Sir Henry, are you ok?"

He pointed at his throat and continued to gasp for air, and he began to turn red with panic. All I could think of doing was the Heimlich Maneuver, so I got behind him and began squeezing his torso, placing pressure on his sternum with my joined fists. It was at this moment of confusion that Reeves burst through the door saying, "Sir Henry, I heard some noise and.... Stop that, what are you doing there?" as he raced to us to try and get me from holding Henry.

Reeves yelled towards the open door, "Thomas, come here at once!" Then, turning his voice on me, stop it I say, and he hit me with his hands first and then, he took a book of the shelf and swatted my head with it.

Thomas entered the door, to join in the fray, but I knew I had to keep pressing Henry's sternum, so I yelled, "He swallowed the biscuit and started choking and"…that's all I remember until I awoke sometime later.

Thomas has used the Room's Fireplace End Iron and hit me with it, whereupon I collapsed on the floor.

CHAPTER 14

FROM HOPE TO DESPAIR?

Upon waking from my instrument induced temporary coma, I could only feel the pain on the side of my head. After keeping my hand on the sore spot of a while I removed it only to notice the blood on my hands, as my wound was still spewing. It was then, I noticed my familiar surroundings, "the stockade", as I lay there in the bed of hay.

No sooner had I wondered what the heck had happened, than the events before my head was hit, became clear to me. In trying to help "flush out" Sir Henry's biscuit, Reeves entrance turned the scene into an attack from me on to Henry, which he and Thomas quickly extinguished, much to the pain on my skull.

Sir Henry, what of Henry? Oh, dear God, I hope he did not choke to death. Because if he did, then in trying to save him from choking, I may have signed my own death warrant. It took me several minutes before I was able to right myself and stand up. As soon as I began walking around in my cell, I heard the keys unlock my chamber door and in entered my two best friends again.

This time they were rougher than ever, I few smacks a piece upon my head, made me fear the worst had happened to Henry. As they tied my hands behind my back, the tightness of the rope immediately began minimizing the blood flow to my hands.

As they dragged me from the Stockade to the house, I began thinking Lisa was right in her fears that I may not return from this trip back in time. Halfway to the house, my two jailers threw a sack over my head. I was I led blindly towards the building. Trying to stay on my feet became a struggle, as my handlers didn't care if I walked or was dragged all the way. Although I couldn't see through the sack, I began hearing our footsteps walking over crushed stones, indicating we were not near the back of the house, but rather to its' side where the carriages would stop. My guess was right, because at that moment, I heard the opening of a carriage door, and seconds later, I lay on the floor of this vehicle. It was not a regular carriage, because I laid sprawled out and at first, I could not reach the side of my new lodgings.

The door was slammed behind me and I heard keys lock the door as well. It was at that moment, that I realized my new lodging was a paddy wagon of sorts; circa 1848.

"And I hope they boil you in oil before they cut off yer 'ead, you maggot!" Came the kind comment from one of my handlers.

With that, I then heard other carriage doors opening and the ensuing conversations… "Please let Lady Elizabeth know, that Windsor will deal harshly and swiftly with this charlatan."

"Thank you so much, Lord Carnarvon. It's a miracle that you just happen to come back this afternoon to help us handle the intruder. Thank goodness Sir Henry appears to be breathing better today. It was touch and go for a while, but the good Doctor, says he should be fine. I'm concerned he doesn't remember the events of yesterday, but if Thomas and I hadn't intervened, who knows what he might have done to the Baronet." Said the relieved Mr. Reeves.

Lord Carnarvon replied, "It turned out to be a blessing that Lady Carnarvon forgot her jewelry when we first left yesterday morning. Remember, when Sir Henry is well enough to recount the incident, he should sign that document I created, as it can be attested by you as a witness, and then, you can just send a courier with the document to the Tower of London, to the attention of Lord Esterlin, Minister of Justice for the Tower. 'Tis all on the paperwork I left on Henry's desk. I am re-routing my return to Highclere, to stop by London and the Tower, and I shall confer with Lord Esterlin, so he will be looking for Sir Henry's Document, before the verdict and sentence are handed out. This seems to be a clear case of a Highwayman trying to get something for nothing from our Sir Henry. Nothing since the likes of Richard Turpin, I'd say."

It was then I heard the knocking on my carriage door and him yelling at me inside, "When you are ready to claim your guilt, just shout out to us." As Carnarvon got into his coach, he shouted instruction to the two carriage drivers, "Remember, make haste drivers, perhaps we can jostle our passenger into a confession before we reach London."

After getting inside his coach, Carnarvon waved out the window and said, "Thank you Reeves. Please send me updates on Henry's condition. I shall be at Highclere for the next month."

"Will do my Lord. Safe travels." Replied Reeves, waving to the carriages as they turned towards the exit of the Broome Park Estate.

What lay ahead of me, I could not say. But it was certain, I was headed away from Broome Park and any chance at getting into the Fog and back to Lisa. If I correctly interpreted Lord Carnarvon's comments to Reeves, I was on my way to trial and execution at The Tower of London. What else could his words have meant.

What I didn't understand or even know about, is Sir Henry's condition. Had I successfully pressured his sternum to release the bits of biscuit in his windpipe, or did it happen naturally once Thomas knocked me out? Was Henry conscious or in a coma, unable to tell anyone what truly transpired in his office yesterday.

Yesterday? I began to think about my conversations with Henry. I knew it was about

5:00pm when we were in our discussion. From the sunlight when I emerged from the stockade, I noticed the setting sun, so evidently, the blow to my head left me unconscious for almost 27-28 hours. The hunger in my stomach confirmed that estimate. And then, the jostling Cararvon had ordered was beginning to happen.

The ride from the house to the estate's exit was slightly downhill and winding, so the coach drivers, handled that portion of our trip with care. However, I felt us turning Westward onto the road to London, and the speed of both coaches picked up significantly. Not that any of my traveling companions cared, but trying to stay right side up, while on the floor of a paddy wagon, with your hands tied behind your back and a hood over your head, did not make for an enjoyable journey. If I were to survive the trip, I knew I had to stabilize myself….but how?

The last right turn of the coach, slid me over to a corner of the floor, so I braced myself, by placing my left foot on the front wall of my carriage and my right foot on the floor, to prevent me from sliding from side to side. With this position, my head was against the side wall of the coach, and with this, I rubbed my head against the wall in hopes that the hood would slide off my head. I took about a dozen rubs, coupled with my teeth holding the inside of the hood in place, allowing for partial removal of the hood to continue. Finally, I succeeded, and even though I was beginning to be thrown around by the coach going over bumps in the road, at least having the ability to see, made it less frightening than doing it blindly.

With each turn I slid from side to side and with my hands, even tied behind me, I was able to handle the bumps in the road, cushioning the bouncing on my tail bone. Two small carriage windows, with an opening of 2 inches high and 6 inches long, allowed at least what remained of the daylight to spill into my black painted traveling stockade. However, there was no straw to provide any cushion to the ride.

I still needed to get my hands untied. But how? As I said before, my land jailers had tightly tied the rope around my hands. I eventually remembered my wristwatch and I managed to remove it from my wrist, as I was able to place it between two fingers of my right hand. My thought was to use the "strap pin", which was used to key the wrist band in place, so that if I could penetrate the rope with the pin, it might eventually poke a hole into the rope and somehow unravel the strands to the point where additional wrist maneuvering could free me.

This worked for a while, as I could feel the pin in place on the rope. However, a severe bump in the road, halted my progress and I lost the grip of the watch and watchband. After the road had straightened, I managed to locate my sliding watch and re-gripped it into position and continued my attempt.

It took about an hour or so, but eventually, enough of a tear in the rope occurred to allow my wrists to wriggle enough to set me free. By this time, there was almost no light coming through my coach windows, but I was able to feel my blood, which was trickling up my arms; a result of the pin sticking me, from time to time, rather than the rope. But I was grateful, as now the night road, became even bumpier, as the drivers couldn't anticipate potholes in the road.

Even the horses objected after a while, and the pace of our journey slowed to sane rate. I could hear the drivers talking to each other and Lord Carnarvon, stating the dark road was too dangerous to go any faster. Upon this discussion,

I also overheard Lady Carnarvon saying, "Who cares if we get a confession from the man, let's not kill ourselves in the process." With that, the journey became a slow clip clop pace throughout the night.

Finally, finding a position with my back against the front wall of my cage and my feet slightly braced against the side wall, I managed to fall asleep. For how long, I wasn't certain, because when I awoke, it was still very dark. The only sounds were the horses' hooves on the dirt road, and the wheels of the coach keeping rhythm with the creaks and moans that the carriages themselves were making. Occasionally, the Carnarvon coach driver would yell to his Footman, who would yell to my driver, "Turn left coming up, or going downhill for a while now."

Then, as quickly as the dark had come, light began to make its' way through my small windows, indicating that dawn was approaching. I remember hearing Lord Carnarvon's driver say to my driver, that it would be about an 8-hour ride at night, from Sir Henry's Estate to the outskirts of London. After that, it would be another good 30-40 minutes to get to the London Bridge, cross it and make our way to our final destination.

For a while, I let my fears get the best of my, as I began to imagine the horrors that might await me at The Tower. I was suddenly recalling television shows or movies, in which the Tower was used as a place of torture for too many of its' residents, both commoner and Royalty. The Tower made no distinction between Classes, but merely carried out the wishes of those who make the ultimate decisions over its' inmates.

Would there be a trial? Would I be tortured until the trial or left alone in a dungeon? How long would it take Sir Henry to awake from his coma, if indeed he was to ever awake. If that was the case, would I be forgotten in the dungeon until some communication from Broome Park or Highclere gave my fate some other alternative?

My only hope seemed to be a quick and complete recovery by Sir Henry, so he could tell others exactly what caused him to begin choking and that I was only trying to help him with the Heimlich Maneuver. Or would he even think that? Perhaps, he thought, in his current state of choking, that I was trying to accelerate the choking? After all, I have no idea if Henry had ever heard of the Heimlich procedure. Who the hell was Heimlich in the first place?

Our conversations were going so well with Sir Henry and he seemed truly delighted listening to me tell him about the future of our world. My only concern at that point, was, once Henry freed me, how was I going to get back to Lisa. And I began to miss my kids, Alex, Deidra and Cheryl very much. How foolish this was for me to do. Even if I escaped or were to be pardoned, the challenge of returning to the future remained.

It was still August and the weather forecast for County Kent, was for another few days of heavy fog from Dover to Canterbury. Would there be any fog at this time in 1848? Going back the first time, was easy because I was only caught in 1943 for a brief time, and that was only as a listener. Had I used up my available time with my stay at Broome Park? Was I destined to become a 19th Century resident, or would destiny allow me to return to 2022? Why, oh why, did I have to be curious? Why couldn't I leave well enough alone? After all, Lisa had witnessed the testimonies of the Witherington's, and the Mayfield's, so we could certainly recant my experiences to Mom and Dad and our Kids and prove to all, that I did go back in time. Why the second time, when

Lisa so rightly objected to its' possibilities of my not returning.

"There it 'tis Edgar. Tis only an hour until we cross the bridge." Came the words of our travel status from the Footman of our first coach.

"You're right about that Bartholomew. At's a good lad, you are." Replied Edgar as he continued, "Is the Master and the Misses still sleeping?"

"No, we're not Edgar. We just awakened and Lady Carnarvon would like to stop soon." Turning his voice to his driver, "Timothy, how far to the Estermore tavern?"

Timothy immediately replied, "Only minutes away your Grace. Just down the next hill and to the right a bit. Their proprietor should be stirring by now."

"Thank you, Timothy." Said the Lord in relief. "Only a short time away my dear."

All were correct, because it was only 5 minutes later by my watch, when I peeked out my side window, and saw that the carriages were coming to a stop. Seconds later, emerging from this two-story Tavern-Lodging Facility, came a large burly man, dressed in a cook's outfit. He approached the lead coach, as he awaited the Footman's opening of the left door.

"Here we are your Grace's. Estermore's Tavern." Said the Footman.

"Thank you, Bartholomew," said the Earl, as he exited the coach. He extended his hand to his Wife, "Come my dear, you can freshen up a bit and we can get something to eat and drink here, before the last leg of our trip."

"Hello, your Grace, I am Estermore," came the proprietor's greeting to his early morning customers. "Welcome to my establishment. We have a very nice washroom for my Lady to freshen up. Right this way."

Lady Carnarvon exited the carriage, not looking her usual beautiful self, but then, who would after a night's ride. "Please go with Mr. Estermore dear. And Estermore, please some food for our Coachmen and Footman, and you might as well find some scraps for our prisoner in Coach two." Stated the Earl.

"Edgar let's see how our companion is doing. Please open his door but mind you for any of his tricks." Warned the Earl.

"Will do your Lordship. We won't allow any shenanigans from our cargo." Said Edgar as he opened the lock with one hand, while holding his gun on the opening with the other. "Out you come. You baddun! What's this? How'd you get out of your hood and rope ties. Careful your Grace, this one's a sly one, he is. No tricky stuff now, or else we'll end your life right here. You're a prisoner of her Majesty so act accordingly. Step down slowly."

With my bloodied hands in the air, I stepped out into the morning light as best I could, stumbling to the ground, I didn't move any more until told to do so.

"How'd you get your hands out of those ties, they told me they tied them ever so tight. And the Hood as well. Are you some type of magician?" Said Edgar.

"Now Edgar, our prisoner is not going to give us any trouble are you sir?" Said the Earl, as he reached in his carriage to retrieve his pistol and pointed it at me.

"Absolutely not your Grace." I said. "I merely tried removing my binds and the hood, to keep me from being hurt on the ride. You can re-tie my hands if you like. I meant no hard to anyone, especially Sir Henry. Can you please tell me how you left him?"

"Never you mind about Sir Henry. Reeves stopped you from your attempted murder, and for that my friend, you will hang at the Tower. All we need is for Sir Henry's recovery and his testimony to reach London. But, if he doesn't recover, Reeves sworn testimony will ensure you receive due justice. Back in the coach for now. We will bring you some food. We're an hour from the Tower. Back in you go." Said the Earl, as his gun was firmly placed in my back.

"Will there be a trial?" I yelled out the coach window, trying to open the discussion.

"You will be given a fair trial. After all, this is England and we allow, even our worst of attempted Murderers to have their time in court." Smiled Lord Carnarvon and as he walked into the tavern. It was then, that Esterton returned with a plate for me, which he slid under the locked door. They were right about one thing, these scraps looked like something a dog would reject, but my hunger overruled my senses and I ate everything within a few seconds.

CHAPTER 15

SIR HENRY'S "DELICATE CONDITION"

While the journey to London continued, life back at Broome Park centered around Sir Henry. Elizabeth had not left his side all night. He was breathing comfortably but still had not awakened from his coma.

A knock and the door opened, as it brought Reeves into Sir Henry's bed chamber, with Lady Elizabeth in the chair beside his bed. "How is his Lord doing my Lady?" Asked Reeves.

"He seems comfortable Reeves, but nothing more." She replied

"The good Doctor has awakened and will be here momentarily my Lady." Reeves added.

"Thank you, Reeves." She said.

"Ah, here he is now. Shall I get you anything my Lady?" Reeves inquired.

"Yes. I would like some tea please." Was her reply as she changed focus to the Doctor and Sir Henry. "He has been breathing fine and uninterrupted Doctor Gains, but shouldn't he be awakening soon?"

"Your Grace. It is hard to know exactly what happened with Sir Henry." Said Gains.

"You heard Reeves and Thomas's account. He was trying to choke Sir Henry." Said Elizabeth.

"My only concern my Lady is for Sir Henry, and in examining his body after we stabilized his breathing yesterday, I did not discover any evidence of strangulation on his neck. I did, however, notice slight bruising on the middle of his chest. My Lady, do you recall anything before yesterday that might have caused this to happen?" Stated the Doctor.

"No nothing along those lines Doctor." Said Elizabeth. "But you yourself said he was being choked."

"Not exactly, your Ladyship." Said Gains. What I said, was the Sir Henry showed signs inside of his throat that he had been choking.

And, I found some crums of the biscuits which Reeves had brought his Grace, along with the Champagne. When I asked Reeves about the biscuits, he stated he noticed and picked up a "wet" piece of a biscuit from the floor of the room, as he was cleaning up the mess from the struggle."

"Couldn't the man have attempted to do his evil, as Henry was eating the biscuit and drinking the champagne?" Asked Elizabeth.

"Yes, that is possible, but upon asking Reeves the "condition of the biscuit", asking if it was flaky and coming apart, as biscuits do, he stated that the wet biscuit was like a clump of already chewed food, wet with the Champagne and/or saliva." Stated the Doctor.

"What is it you're saying Doctor? Could Henry have been choking on the food, rather than being choked by the intruder?" She asked.

"My Lady, things are a bit confusing here. First of all, if the intruder was trying to harm to Sir Henry, why didn't he do like Thomas did, and just use the End Iron to hit Henry? It wasn't like he was being able grab anything of value and run out the door and escape. Most all the staff was nearby, and this Mr. Christian, would have known trying to do Henry harm, would be to no avail. And, didn't Reeves first say, that Henry and Mr. Christian seemed to be getting along fine. After all, Sir Henry ordered Champagne, which seems like maybe they were toasting something from their conversations together?" The Doctor pondered. "It just doesn't add up to an attempted murder. Plus, the fact, that when Reeves and Thomas were trying to separate the Man from Henry, they stated he kept his arms around the torso of Henry. Perhaps, that might explain the slight bruises on Henry's chest. A brawl and attempt to murder Henry, just doesn't seem logical to me."

"Well now that you mention this, when Henry first met with the man two days ago, Henry relayed to me, that Christian, claimed to be a distant relative of mine. Me, Elizabeth!" She said. "I guess there may be some other explanation to the situation. It all happened so fast."

"What do you mean it all happened so fast." Asked Gains.

"Reeves came into the parlor and stated that Henry and Mr. Christian, seemed to be getting on so well, and that I was to be called into the room for further explanation. Then, Lord Carnarvon came back, unexpectedly." She said.

"I thought he was here all the time, celebrating with You and Henry?" He asked.

They were all here for two days, and except for my Sister Mary and Her Friend, everyone else from the wedding party, who had ridden down from London, had left only 30 minutes or so, before Henry and Mr. Christian began their discussion." Explained Elizabeth.

"Why did he return?" He asked.

"Lady Carnarvon had forgotten she had placed her jewelry in a bottom draw of their bedroom, and they had ridden only a few miles, when it dawned on her, and they returned, just as the fray in the study began." She said. "The Earl kind of took over things, as he had been told by Henry, the night before, that Mr. Christian, seemed a charlatan and up to no good, so Lord Carnarvon just assumed the worst, and had Reeves send our Driver, by Horse, to Canterbury to get a Jailer's Wagon, to take Mr. Christian to The Tower of London for Trial and Sentencing. At the time, Reeves and Thomas' testimony seemed to be all the justification the Earl needed for ordering the carriage. Now, I don't know. What do you think Doctor?"

"Perhaps, Lady Elizabeth, just perhaps, our

intruder, was NOT trying to do harm to Henry, but rather, he was trying to help Henry." He proposed.

"What do you mean, help Henry?" She asked.

"Look at it this way. Henry was in duress, either from Mr. Christian or on his own. When Reeves and Henry entered, why didn't Mr. Christian try to fight them off? Instead, he kept, as Thomas stated, "Squeezing Henry", right up to the time that Thomas hit Jensen in the head with the End Iron." The Doctor stated.

"Why? So, as to squeeze out the food on which Henry may have been choking?" She asked.

"I recently read a medical article from Germany. The Doctor who wrote it, talked about a layman's procedure for helping someone who is choking. You get behind the choke victim and place your hands on the breastplate of the victim and squeeze and squeeze, and this creates pressure inside the lungs, which may "force out" any obstacle in the breathing tube of the victim." Said the Doctor, as he stared at Elizabeth.

"Oh, dear God. Doctor, Mr. Christian may have been trying to save Henry, as you say. What should we do?" She asked.

With that, Henry began to stir in his bed.

"Henry?" Said Elizabeth. "Oh Henry, you're ok." As Henry's eyes opened, he took an exceptionally large breath and then, retracted in pain.

"Sir Henry, what is it." The Doctor asked.

Without saying anything, Henry pointed to his chest, to the middle of his chest. The Doctor then opened Henry's pajama top to reveal to Henry and Elizabeth, the bruise on his chest. "Sir Henry. You have a bruise on your chest. How did it get there?"

After gathering himself and sitting up a little, letting us know he was alright, he began, "My good friend, and your Nephew my Dear, Mr. Christian. I was choking on the biscuit and he squeezed me and then I fainted. Where is Mr. Christian?" Asked Henry. "I want to thank him."

The Doctor immediately walked out of the parlor, asking for Reeves. Elizabeth bent over in tears and hugged Henry. "I'm ok my dear. No need to cry. How long have I been out?" asked Henry.

Meanwhile, back in London. Lord Carnarvon's Carriage and the Prisoner's Wagon have made their way across London Bridge and turned towards The Tower of London.

Coachman Timothy steering the horses to

the Tower entrance calls out to Lord Carnarvon, "We're here your Grace. What shall we do with the other coach?" asked Timothy.

Exiting the Coach, the Earl, said to the Lady, "My Dear, we shall only be here a few minutes, I will need to sign a few documents, and hand over the prisoner to Lord Esterlin. He shant like this prisoner very much, because his Father, was great friends with Sir Henry's Father, the 7th Baronet. Quick justice is likely to follow."

"Oh, please my Dear, do hurry, I just hate the thought of being near this horrid place." Cried Lady Carnarvon.

With that the Earl, gave his credentials to the Guardsmen, and asked to be escorted to Lord Esterlin, and informed the guard, of the attempted murderer in the jailer's carriage.

"We will handle his likes, your Grace. Lord Esterlin just came in a few minutes ago." Stated one of the Tower's Guardsman.

Upon reaching the Tower Offices, the Chief Guardsman, with military precision, began his introduction, "His Lordship, The Earl of Carnarvon, to see his Grace, Lord Esterlin."

With such a loud introduction, the door to Esterlin's office opened and out came James

Esterlin. "Henry. How are you my friend. What brings the 3rd Earl of Carnarvon and Highcleer to The Tower of London?"

As they embrace, "James, I am well my friend. I trust all is well with you. However, I am here on important business from Broome Park."

"And how is Sir Henry Oxenden?" Asked James.

"Unfortunately, Sir James, our mutual friend, was assaulted by an intruder to Broome Park, and had it not been for his Butler Reeves and others, Sir Henry might have met his doom. When I left there not 8 hours ago, he was still not conscious, but under a Doctor's care." Explained the Earl.

"Then I assumed you captured the charlatan and are here to place him in my Tower." Replied Sir James.

"Precisely." As the Earl handed James his documents. "I had the papers signed by witnesses and if Sir Henry is revived, he will sign his account of the attempted murder, and a courier will deliver it as soon as possible."

As he reviewed the papers, James looked up at the Earl and stated, "Your Lordship, I do not see the necessity of receiving Sir Henry's own version. If Sir Henry doesn't pull through to the point where he can document the attack, your papers here are clearly enough to put this intruder to death. Where and Who is he?"

"His name, as it says on Mr. Reeves' statement, is Mr. Evan Christian, who happened on the Broome Park Property 3 days ago. I was at Broome Park to celebrate the Wedding of Sir Henry. We left two days ago, but Lady Carnarvon and I returned because she had forgotten some items, and it was upon our return that the attempt on Sir Henry was in the process. Once ordered was restored, I summoned a Jailer Carriage from Canterbury, and that driver, carriage and suspect are in your courtyard. I would stay around a little longer, but Lady Carnarvon and I are long overdue at Highcleer and we must depart immediately. So, my friend, I leave this in your hands. Thank you." Said the Earl.

"Let me escort you out Sir Henry." James said. The two walked through the garrison and towards the courtyard to the carriage.

They shook hands and the Earl, tapped on the door of the carriage and bid farewell to me. "Mr. Christian, may your soul be forgiven for what you did. Goodbye."

He departed joining Lady Carnarvon and

as their carriage pulled away from The Tower, Sir James Esterlin began his taunts. "You, my misguided young man, will gain no quarter from me. Sir Henry's Father, the 7th Earl, was my Father's Best Friend. I shall enjoy watching you die. Take him to Cell 1 and begin the scheduling." He said to his Guardsmen.

CHAPTER 16

THE RACE TO SAVE ME

Sitting in a moving jail has a sense of freedom to it, because it's likely that nothing will happen to you until you reach your destination. Not so with a regular jail.

As Sir James Esterlin and his Guardsmen escorted me to my cell, I think on purpose, they took the long way to get there, as I was routed through several floors, as they ensured I saw the various torture implements used at the Tower. Then, we went into the lower floor of the Tower and past the cells of tenants who looked as though they had been there for years. What is surprising about this technique to scare, is that it contradicted everything I knew about Sir Henry

Oxenden, the 7th Baronet of Broome Park, and if Sir James was correct, with his Father being best friends with Sir Henry the 7th, it didn't add up. Perhaps the current Sir James, wasn't like his Father and thought he would bring justice to the world to put to death bad guys. Or perhaps, after being the resident in charge of the Tower, the horror of this place rubbed off on him and he enjoys seeing others suffer.

In any case, when I reached my cell, I was experiencing a mixture of fear, disbelief and a calmness that things would work out. How, I wasn't quite sure? I couldn't comprehend the events of the past 72 hours without thinking that Lisa was still waiting for me. Was it 72 hours later in 2022, or was time passing in limbo for her as she passed the time wandering the gardens of Broome Park.

I also began thinking of Sir Henry the 8th and his battle overcoming his choking. Was he dead? Was he still in a coma and what was Lady Elizabeth thinking about her new husband? Little did I know that efforts were under way to save me.

"Hurray Edmond. Remember use the money to drop off your current horse to buy a new one. We will send follow up riders to retrieve our horses and buy them new horses. You have Sir Henry's seal as proof. Then get to Sir James Esterlin at the Tower and deliver this message from Sir Henry to him as soon as you can. God's Speed." Cried Lady Elizabeth, and she waved to Broome Park's best Horseman, as he headed due Northwest towards London to save Mr. Christian.

She then, turned towards Reeves saying again, "It is not your fault. I know you were just trying to save Sir Henry. Right now, we need to save Mr. Christian. I pray to God that Edmond will get there in time with the signed note and seal from Sir Henry stating Mr. Christian's innocence. For now, we need to get Sir Henry and Me and You in our Carriage and get to London."

"We will leave immediately your Ladyship. All is packed for you and Sir Henry and our Coachmen and Footman will get you there quickly." Said Reeves. With that Henry walked out the front door of Broome Park and into the waiting coach and off they went. It would likely be 6 hours before our "daylight coach" would reach London but Edmond should be able to be there in 3 hours. God willing.

CHAPTER 16-A

MY LAST DAY

Visions of Lisa, Alex, Deidra and Cheryl was all that was going through my mind, when the Tower Guards, opened my cell and placed down next to me, a metal plate and mug. They had put my hands in chains, when I first entered the cell. The length of the chains allowed me to get up and walk around my 8' by 6' new residence. The ceiling was only about 5' tall, and besides the wooden jail door, which had a small sliding window contained 4 feet above the ground, there was no other place to let any light make its' way into my cell. In other words, it was dark.

My guess was that I was about 2 stories below the level of the street entrance to the Tower, which would put me at about water level to the Thames, where I remember seeing TV and/or movie shows, in which the Tower of London was used for both its' good and nefarious purposes. Prisoners who were transported to the Tower via boat, would come through the "Tower's water gate", with its' ominous looking doorway. It was plain and simple; The Tower was not meant to be a fun experience for its' occupants.

I wondered if the "chopping block" they took me past, might be used for my head. That would be quick and immediate, as opposed to the "racks", which seemed much more painful to endure. Stretching someone's bones and muscles to the point of ripping them apart, didn't give me the happiest of thoughts. Yet, somehow, it was strange. I had a sense that I was going to be rescued, but how and when, eluded my self-explanation.

So, with all my surroundings, I sat down next to my food stuffs to perhaps eat my last meal, which was more of a beefless stew, with a few vegetables serving as my nutritional value for the day. Actually, this food tasted better than the meal given me while I was traveling from Broome Park to London. However, the Tower's accommodations proved less favorable. I was here waiting for trial, but what of Sir Henry?

"Oh, dear Elizabeth," cried out Henry as he and Reeves and Lady Elizabeth rocked back and forth in their face paced carriage, along the road towards London, "If anything should happen to Mr. Christian, I could never forgive myself."

"We will get there in time Henry. Edmond should only be about an hour away from the Tower, as we speak." Comforted his wife.

"My Lord, I don't know how not to take the blame for all that has happened." Explained Reeves.

"Reeves, please do not feel that way. I know you were only acting to protect me, and I'm sure, it certainly appeared nefarious." Replied Henry, as he continued writing a letter, despite the bumpy conditions. "There, I've finished the note to the Earl, explaining the truth of this issue, and informing him, I appreciated his reactions and actions, because, after all, in his shoes, I would have likely reacted the same way. I hold him no malice and informed him, that we will let him know of Mr. Christian's plight."

The Lady replied, "But, Henry, won't the Earl be at the Tower?"

"Not likely my Dear," said Henry, "He needed to get back to Highcleer as he was already delayed, so I imagined he dropped off the witnessed documents with Sir James, and then left. I can only hope James will take the case through due process and not rush to judgment and sentencing. I pray he will not." Henry gazed out the carriage window, hoping his wish will come true.

"We're three hours away ourselves, your Grace." Reeves interjected, "With God's Grace, all will be well." And, with those thoughts, the three passengers sat quietly for the remainder of their journey.

"Now then, Mr. Christian." Declared the Head Guard, "Sir James is ready for you. I hope you enjoyed your last meal?" As he escorted me, out of my cell and down the corridor, through two sets of heavy wooded, double doors. As we walked through the second set, another hallway emerged, but this one was drastically different than the dungeon hallway. It looked more like a government building hallway, adorned with framed pictures of people, who looked like "officials". Perhaps, these were the past Heads of The Tower. None of the pictures contained faces with smiles, but rather, stern looking, well dressed, important people, like Sir James.

The right walls of this hallway, contained an

occasional leaded glass window, providing a view to the Tower's courtyard of sorts, with sidewalks, flower beds and a few trees adorning the open space of this dismal place.

Another 50 feet and we turned left, through another set of doors, into, what appeared to be, a Courtroom, adorned with a place for the Judge up front, and a box, off to the right of the judge's seat, which is where they led me, still with my hands and feet in chains.

"Sit there and await your judgment." Came the Guard's stern directions.

Looking around this room, I noticed only a few other, comfortably looking chairs, perhaps for visiting dignitaries, or key witnesses, either spectating, or awaiting their turn to provide evidence to the court. Following us into the room, were several well-dressed soldiers, looking more like the Guards at Buckingham Palace, than jailers. Their bright red coats were adorned with lapels and "other lettuce", offering the conclusion, that their position at The Tower of London, was one of importance.

They assumed their assigned stations, and stood erect, and became even more erect, when the one of them, posted the closest to the Judge's bench, pounded his rifle on the wood floor of the courtroom, as he announced to the room's occupants, "All Stand!", He paused and once again, slammed his rifle on the floor. "His Royal Appointee, Sir James Esterlin, Master in Charge of Her Majesty's Court at The Tower of London. All give Sir James his due respect." With that, the door to the left of the Judge's bench opened, with Lord Esterlin walking through, wearing courtly looking black robes, with his head adorned, with a plush looking, felt hat, twice the size of his head, and containing several tassels hanging from the back of the hat.

This was indeed going to be my trial. The only thing that appeared to be missing was someone who would be appointed to defend me. With that, Sir James reached his bench, and sat. The designated, Sergeant at Arms, again hammered his rifle, and all others seated themselves, save the standing guards, still as rigid as ever.

From his seated position, a rather small, timid looking, but officially dressed man, approached the front of the room, turning towards Esterlin, as he began, "Hear ye, hear ye, all here draw near and be heard in Her Majesty's Court, in the Matter of the Crown, against, Mister Evan Christian, a vagrant, accused of attempted Murder, against a Royal Patron of England, Sir Henry Chudleigh Oxenden, the 8th Baronet of Broome Park, Barham, County Kent, England. Having said his peace, the Court Official, then placed some papers on the Judge's desk and returned to his assigned seat, where he took some paper and a twill pen, preparing to write.

After a period of silence, and a review of the documents in front of him, Sir James removed his glasses, and glared at me. The silence was deafening, as the Judge began, "Why are you still standing?" With that, I sat on the edge of the box, as there was no seat on which to seat. "Get up, he yelled." Causing me to quickly re-stand. "You are on trial for your life and you will remain standing until this hearing is complete. Please state your name and place of residence."

Not expecting to talk so soon, I cleared my throat and began, "Your Highness…."

"I am not of Royal Blood. You will address me as Judge, or Sir James, or Lord Esterlin." Retorted the man in charge, who was already agitated before my verbal snafu.

"I am very sorry Sir James." I said, trying to gather my composure. "My name is Evan

Christian and I am from the State of Michigan, in the United States of America."

Sir James, remained quiet again, and re-looked at his documents, and then back at me, as he continued, "You mean to propose to me, that you have come to England, from across the Atlantic Ocean, and were just walking through the center of County Kent, without a single possession with you, save the clothes on your back, and you expect this court to believe you're an American?"

"Judge, I know my being at Broome Park may appear unusual to this court, but if you would ask Sir Henry, he will tell you that…" I tried to explain, until Esterlin interjected, "Sir Henry, whom you tried to choke to death, and were it not for his Butler, you would be on trial for murder, rather than attempted murder? I have sworn testimony from Mr. Reeves, Head Butler at Broom Park, who witnessed your attack and with his efforts and that of Broome Park's footman, Thomas, they subdued you and in turn, they saved the life of Sir Henry."

"But that's not what happened Sir James." I tried to explain.

"So, now you are calling these witnesses liars?" Angrily stated the Judge. "We shall add slander to your list of charges." Picking up the papers on his desk, "These Mr. Christian, are not falsely prepared documents, but rather, official texts of first hand witnesses, who conferred their statements to Sir Henry, the 3rd Earl of Carnarvon, who in turn, delivered them, AND YOU, to this Tower for the purpose of allowing you to admit your guilt. But, if you insist on lying to this court, we need no longer delay the court's indulgence, and go right to sentencing."

"But Lord Esterlin, you haven't heard the whole truth. Please let me explain. I am from the future." Was all that I could think of in my defense.

"The FUTURE!" Yelled Sir James. This is preposterous and your time is over. It is the judgment of this court, that you are guilty as charged and you will be hung by the neck until you are dead, as soon, as these proceedings are over!"

With that, I fainted.

Not knowing how much time transpired from my fainting until I awoke in my cell, when my eyes opened, I looked up, into the smiling eyes of two of my jailers, who began, "Sylvester," he yelled out the door, "Go and tell Lord Esterlin, he has awakened."

In the background, I hear footsteps turn into running, as both jailers, picked me up, dragging me through the cell door, and down the hallway. "Up, get up you snake. You thought you would avoid experiencing the noose by falling asleep. Not here at the Tower. We make sure all executed here are awake and aware during their hanging, which is where you are headed, right now!"

I walked as best I could, but they kept my pace brisk, as they seemed to be looking forward to my demise. We went out the dungeon hallway, through a tunnel, and then left, up steps, and through two steel doors, and out into the Tower Courtyard. They paused, allowing me to take in my surroundings, which, as I panned the scene, I saw the full grounds of England's most terrible place. Halfway through my viewing, I saw the gallows, with the rope hanging there just awaiting my neck. With that, they commenced my final steps, and it was then, that I realized now I had to make my peace with God, so, I began my thoughts, "Our Father, Who art in heaven, Hallowed be Thy Name."

Up the steps, they led me towards the hangman,

whose head was covered in a black hood, with two eyes holes, so that I would not be able to know the face of the person, who would actually pull the hangman's rope lever. I continued, "Give us this Day, our Daily Bread, and forgive me my trespasses, as I need to forgive those who would trespass against me." He placed the rope around my neck and tightened the noose. "Lead me not into temptation but deliver me from evil."

Then, not having even noticed the presence of Sir James Esterlin, his voice got my attention, "Are there any final words, you wish to say to this court?"

Looking towards heaven, all I could say was, "Lord, please forgive my arrogance with investigated Broome Park, and please take care of Lisa, Alex, Deidra and Cheryl, for I love them Lord." I then, bowed my head and continued praying.

It is the sentence of this court, that you, Evan Christian, having been found guilty with the attempted murder of Sir Henry Oxenden, will be hung by your neck, this day, until you are dead. May God in Heaven have mercy on your sole. Then, turning towards the hangman to give the final sign, raising his hand.......

"WAIT, WAIT, STOP, STOP the Hanging," Came the cry from the Tower's office doorway. "He is innocent. Mr. Christian is innocent. Sir Henry is alive and well and he is on his way here as I speak. I am Edmond, servant of Sir Henry, who has sent me to you Sir James to stop these proceedings." With that, and finishing his run to Sir James' side, Edmond continued, "Your Grace. He is innocent. Please stop the hanging. Sir Henry is in his coach hours behind me but he is coming here to testify." Then Edmond collapsed from exhaustion on the ground next to James, still reaching out to Esterlin to believe him.

Hearing the words of Edmond, I sank to my knees and said, "Thank you God. Thank you."

Back in my cell, alone and still crying, I couldn't help but say to God, please forgive me for not believing you would save me. My tears sustained me and allowed the time to pass, until the jailer's keys found my cell door, whose click, turned my tears to smiles. The verbal demeanor of my guards had also changed. While they stopped short of apologizing, they did say, "It's nice to see someone, so close to death, to be exonerated of their crime. It doesn't happen here my friend.

You are one lucky American. Are you really an American?" They asked.

Walking down the hallway, I smiled at them and said, "As unlikely as it may seem to you, I am indeed an American."

The doors to the courtyard opened and there before me, crying and smiling was Sir Henry, my 6th time Great Aunt and an even greater smiling Reeves, all welcoming me with open arms.

"Sorry Evan. We are so sorry." Said Henry, as he hugged me like a brother.

CHAPTER 17

NOW, HOW DO I GET BACK TO LISA?

After the ride back to Broome Park from London, driving up the entrance way to Henry's Family Estate, seemed more at home than as a visitor who stumbled across this fantastic place a short 4 days ago. The colors of the gardens seemed more vivid and welcoming. The edifice itself took on a new meaning for me, as rather than a sight Uncle Patrick wanted me to see, I somehow knew Uncle Pat wanted me to "experience" Broome Park and not just play the future golf course of this magnificent property.

Pulling up to the front door, our coach was greeted by the entire house staff, whose smiles meant they had already been told that Edmond's ride and the Masters' Carriage trip were successful. As I stepped out of the Coach, they applauded, and they continued clapping until they followed us into the house.

Once inside, Henry and Elizabeth walked me into the parlor. As we sat down next to the fireplace, which I remember seeing during my initial walk through the House, the day I first played golf, while Lisa was still sightseeing in Canterbury. The family pictures adorning walls on either side of the fireplace, suddenly took on new meaning. I remember seeing them, when Uncle Patrick first showed me a magazine article, from the 1890's, which told of the Estate and its' legacy. The most vivid of the pictures, was that of Sir Henry's Father, the 7th Baronet, Sir Henry. As I starred at the picture, I turned to my host and said, "Henry, he would be so proud of you for what you did yesterday, than any Father has a right. Thank you again my friend."

With tears in his eyes, Henry, who was being hugged at that moment by Elizabeth, smiled back at me, and said, "Thank you Evan." He then stood up and began to walk around the parlor and stated, "Although we would love for you to stay with us forever, we need to help you find your way back to your Lisa."

"Yes," said Elizabeth. "I feel so lucky to have met you and as you suggested to Henry and me, that we keep your secret with us and just live our lives as God intended, "focused on Him". We will help you return to your family. How, we're not sure."

"Evan, while you were asleep in the carriage ride home, I have been giving this a lot of thought and all I could come up with is to send Edmond to Dover, and let him stay there until he sees a storm over the channel, that might generate the heavy fog here in County Kent, which, we hope can have it work its' magic on you, and voila, send you forward 174 years, to your awaiting wife." Turning abruptly towards me, after his verbal suggestions. "What do you think?"

"Sounds good to me." Came my smiling reply. "Now, how about letting me meet those 4 wonderful children you have?"

"Why of course," Cried Elizabeth. "You should meet Henry's children. I've fallen in love with them. Their Mother, Charlotte, did a great job at raising them. Reeves, would you bring in the children to meet their future nephew." Smiled her Lady.

The next two days passed quickly, as Henry and I continued our talks about the future, inventions and family. He didn't want to know too much about his family's future, or about the future of Broome Park. He did however, understand that life in the future would change society and that the aristocracy of the past 500 years was coming to a close. He related it to changes in France with the Louie's and the general populace. We talked about how the United States would become an even closer ally to Great Britain and that for years to come, these two countries would become the envy of the world for their "fair treatment" of the world. It would take two World Wars and the deaths of far too many innocent people, caught in the crosshairs of power hungry, misguided leaders, but those who feared God would come to realize with putting God first, those not doing so, would have chaotic lives; some more so, and even those who put their faith in wealth, would never gained true satisfaction with life.

Why God had allowed me to go back in time, I cannot quite comprehend, but perhaps it was to gain an appreciation of what I have with Lisa and the kids, and trying to do things I shouldn't have, like going back in time, was something not to fool with.

On day three back at Broome Park, Edmond came riding up the entrance of the estate. Thomas, the footman, who happened to be outside looking South, when he noticed Edmond approaching, rushed into the house to tell Sir Henry. We all rushed to the entrance to hear of our weather forecast. With a smiling face, Edmond dismounted and approached Sir Henry.

"Your Grace," He said, "You will be happy to know there's a great storm over the Channel and as I rode away from Dover, I could see it was coming on shore headed North."

"Excellent. Thank you, Edmond." Said Henry.

"I thank you too Edmond." I said.

"We all do Edmond you were so critical in saving Evan's life. We owe you so much." Elizabeth stated. "Please get yourself some food and do some swimming at the Pond before the fog rolls in."

"Thank you, My Lady." He said.

"Well Cousin Evan Christian of America, it appears your time with us is limited, so all we can say is thank you for coming. I would help pack, but with only the clothes you are wearing, you trip shall be light, I pray." Said Elizabeth.

"Let's go into the house everyone," said Henry. "I've something to give Evan to take with him. Sort of a lucky charm. If the God's of Time Travel will allow it to go with you, you will have a keepsake to savor and remember us by."

We relaxed, though I must confess, I was anxious to begin the travel process, not knowing if it would work. Henry gave me his Father's watch; a marvelous time piece, made of gold, and it was still keeping time. "He would want you have it, for keeping alive the Oxenden Family/ Tanner Family Connections for the coming years. He would have been thrilled to talk with you, as I have been. Again, we cannot thank you enough for......"

Reeves entered the room, stating, "Your Lordship, please pardon my interruption, but Edmond just stepped outside and he said you can see the fog coming North over the trees."

"Thank you, Reeves," I said turning to my hosts and hugging them one last time. "I had better hurry. I am going to go to the spot where I was when the fog lifted 5 days ago. Hopefully, that will work. Otherwise, I will see you again, once it lifts."

Having said all we wanted to, I walked out the East house entrance, and surely enough, to the South was that all too familiar, rolling cloud, dark as the sea, coming our way.

"Goodbye my friends and thank you." I said as I waved them goodbye.

"God's speed Evan," Said, Henry. We know it will work. "We shall remember you forever." They all waved as I began to run North. The Broome Park village people were all standing there to my right as I passed by the estate buildings and the stockade. They too waved.

By this time, the fog was over the front boundaries of the property and I am guessing I was on about the third hole of the future golf course. As I passed the small pond that fronted the 3rd green. I turned west towards the small forest I came through four days ago and then towards where the 8th green would be. I remember coming the opposite way after the fog had lifted last week.

Turning to look behind me, the fog had already engulfed Broome Park, so one last wave goodbye was fruitless. I kept running and stopped and turned, just as the fog rushed by me.

Like the times before, I struggle to see beyond a few feet in either direction. Before long, the cold moisture within the fog began to chill me. With no shed to get under and no trees to protect me, and not having the ability to see beyond my outstretched arms, I was truly at God's mercy, as to what would happen next.

What seemed like 10 minutes quickly passed. I found a patch of dirt, not covered with grass, which allowed me to sit and not get wet from the moisture penetrating the grass. I sat motionless for another few moments and prayed, "Dear God, Please, allow me to get back to Lisa. And, thank you for this experience."

As I opened my eyes from prayer, the fog was gone. Completely gone. Looking into the sky and Westward, Northward and Eastward, it was as though no fog was there at all. In fact, the immediate warmth of sunshine hit my back, which was facing South. I stood up and as I turned South, I heard voices yelling, "FORE!"

Just then, a golf ball came whizzing by me, landing not 10 feet in front of me and missing my legs by inches.

Two golfers, running up to me from 100 yards or so away, began apologizing halfway to me. "We are so sorry. We did not see you sitting there when we first hit the ball." One of them said. "Did it hit you?"

"No, no," I said. "And it is I who should apologize for not seeing you and for being where I do not belong. I was just resting for a moment before…."

Then, I noticed all the terrain. The golf course, the shed to the West and Broome Park about a half mile South. "I am all right. Sorry for the intrusion. Enjoy your round." As I began my walk back to the house.

From the angle of the sun, it appeared to be about 3:00 to 4:00 in the afternoon. About the same time, as I departed Henry and Elizabeth 20 minutes ago. Could it be that simple? I was back to the 21st century but was it 2022 and how many days has it been since my departure. I passed the 3rd tee box, 2nd green and fairway and then, I began hearing voices calling me; "Is that you again Mr. Christian?"

It was Abernathy at the 1st tee box, getting ready to deploy another foursome on the course. "It 'tis you sir. Why in the world are you coming this way? I was told you might be out there somewhere on the course and to look for you this afternoon."

"Hello Mr. Abernathy. What afternoon is this?" I inquired.

"It is Friday, the 21st." He replied.

"It's today. Today is the 21st. I left the 21st." Talking to myself.

"Where did you go today?" Asked the starter.

"I was here. I was here all the time. Except for London." Again, to myself.

"You went to London and back today sir?" Puzzled Abernathy.

"My wife." I asked. "Have you seen my wife?

"Why yes sir, after lunch, I saw her walking the gardens by herself, but I believe she may be back in Broome Park at this time." Replied Abernathy.

"Thank you." I said. "Thank you, Abernathy." As I ran to the pro shop entrance and into the building.

"Mr. Christian! Hello!" Came the comment from Olivia behind the counter.

"Yes, Hello Miss….Olivia," I said as I walked through the shop and into the house proper.

"Hello Mr. Christian." Came the smiling voice of Miss Knightley.

"Hello." I said, "Hello again. My wife? Have you seen Lisa?"

"Why yes sir. She came in a while ago and I saw her going up the stairs, so I'm guessing she might be in your room." Said Miss Knightly.

"Thank you." I said, rushing through the dining area and the parlor to the front staircase. "Thank you."

I took the 15 stairs in about 5 steps and my heart was pounding even more then when in my cell at The Tower of London. Down the hall to 302, I knocked and opened the door, with Lisa sitting peacefully in the Queen Anne Chair by the window.

"Evan?" She said, not really surprised to see me so soon. "I guess it didn't work after all, did it? The fog lifted about 40 minutes ago. Where on the course were you?"

"I'm here dear. That's all that matters." I said, as I walked over to her, and kissed and hugged her like never before. "That's all that matters."

"Well my dear." Said Henry, as he and Elizabeth walked outside the front of Broome Park. "Can you believe what happened? I know it is hard to believe, but he was here and now he is gone. I think. I hope. I pray he found his Lisa."

As they walked further to the east of the house, they stopped, looked up into the window of the third floor, far right room of the house. To their amazement, in the window were the figures of two people, embracing.

Elizabeth looked up and said, "Why Henry. It's Cousin Evan!"

Then, Henry said, "It is him."

With that, the vision vanished as they both looked at themselves smiling and Henry said to Elizabeth, "He did and that's all that matters. He, being with his Lisa and You here with me. I love you Miss Tanner. I mean Mrs. Oxenden."

THE END

Printed in Great Britain
by Amazon

35409940R00179